The Hardy Boys®
in
Hunting for Hidden Gold

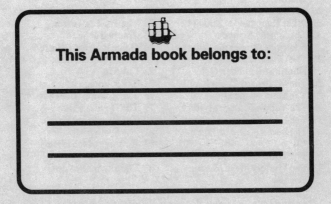

This Armada book belongs to:

_____

_____

_____

Hardy Boys® Mystery Stories in Armada

For contractual reasons, Armada has been obliged to publish from No. 57 onwards before publishing Nos. 43–56. These missing numbers will be published as soon as possible.

The Hardy Boys® Mystery Stories

Hunting for Hidden Gold

Franklin W. Dixon

Armada

First published in the U.K. in 1973 by
William Collins Sons & Co. Ltd, London and Glasgow
First published in Armada in 1976
This impression 1987

Armada is an imprint of
the Children's Division, part of
the Collins Publishing Group,
8 Grafton Street, London W1X 3LA

Printed in Great Britain by
William Collins Sons & Co. Ltd, Glasgow

*The landslide threw the Hardy Boys
from their horses*

CONTENTS

·1·

Danger in the Fog

"SOMEBODY'S going to get hurt!" Frank Hardy exclaimed.

He and his four companions paused in the darkening woods and listened as rifleshots and loud laughter rang out from a nearby ridge.

"Careless hunters," Frank's brother Joe said grimly.

Joe was seventeen, tall and blond, and a year younger than Frank.

"Let's go back to the cabin," urged plump Chet Morton nervously. "I'm hungry, anyhow."

Lanky Biff Hooper agreed. "We can look for a camp-site tomorrow."

"Unless Frank and Joe are called away to solve a mystery," Tony Prito needled.

Frank chuckled. "There's a chance we will—"

Smack! A bullet thudded into a tree an inch from Joe's head!

For a moment there was stunned silence. Then Frank asked quickly, "Joe, are you all right?"

His brother gulped and looked at the gash in the bark. "I'm okay. But one inch closer—"

Biff Hooper's handsome face flushed with anger. "I'm going after those fellows!" he declared.

As he spoke, three hunters came into view.

"Hold it!" Frank hailed them. "You men nearly killed my brother!"

"Why don't you be careful?" Joe shouted.

"Sorry, boys," one of the men called back casually. He and his companions did not stop; instead, they moved on through the undergrowth.

"Is that all you've got to say?" Chet bellowed.

"Forget it, kid," another of the hunters replied. "Nobody got hurt."

"Stupid sportsmen!" growled Joe as the trio disappeared. He added to his companions, "You fellows nearly lost one business partner."

The five boys had pooled money to build their own cabin and were exploring the deep woods north of Bayport looking for a camp-site.

To relieve the tension caused by the near accident, Tony Prito said jokingly, "We're used to the idea of losing you and Frank. Every time we start a project, you two get involved in a mystery."

Frank and Joe were the sons of Fenton Hardy, the well-known detective. They had solved many mysteries on their own and sometimes co-operated with their father in his cases.

Biff grinned. "Amazing! We've been here one whole day, and you Hardys are still with us!"

Frank winked at Joe. "We may have to leave," he admitted. "Dad's on a case out West and we're hoping we'll get a call to go and help him."

The others groaned, then laughed. "In fact," Joe added, "we might even find a clue right around here."

"What!" chorused the Hardys' pals.

"Remember when Frank and I inquired at the store about a man named Mike Onslow?" Joe went on, "Dad asked us to keep an eye out for him. Onslow lives somewhere in these woods, and he may have some useful information that ties in with Dad's case."

"Come on," said Chet. "Let's eat and talk later."

The boys pushed on through the growing darkness. Fog was beginning to rise by the time they reached the edge of the clearing where their rented cabin stood. As they crossed to the crude log house, rifleshots sounded in the distance.

Chet winced. "Those careless hunters are still at it," he remarked.

The boys were about to enter the cabin when Joe exclaimed, "Quiet!"

They all halted, listening intently. "It sounded like a cry," Joe said.

The others had heard nothing, and finally went inside.

"Hope nobody was shot by those fools," Tony remarked, lighting the oil lamp.

Frank and Joe built a fire in the fireplace, while Chet started supper on a wood stove.

"This is a bad place to get hurt," Biff said.

The boys were ten miles from the nearest town, Clintville, and the only road was steep and rutted. They had borrowed Mr Hardy's car for the trip, but had left it in the Clintville Garage. George Haskins, owner of the town's one hotel, had rented them the cabin, and his son Lenny had driven the boys to it in his jeep.

"It wouldn't be easy to get help here," Joe agreed.

"Dinner's nearly ready," Chet announced. "Bring chairs to the—" He stopped short. From the clearing outside came the sound of running feet and then a frantic hammering on the door. Tony strode over and opened it. Lenny Haskins, a lanky boy, stood in the doorway, panting.

"What's the matter?" Tony asked the youth.

"Frank and Joe Hardy have a long-distance call at the hotel," the boy blurted, out of breath.

"From where?" Frank asked.

"Don't know," Lenny said. "There's trouble on the line and all I could make out was that the person would call back in an hour or so."

"Maybe it's Dad!" Frank exclaimed.

"I'll bet you're right," Joe agreed. "We told him he could reach us through Mr Haskins."

"You fellows go ahead and eat," said Frank. "Joe and I will return to the hotel with Lenny."

With the Haskins boy leading the way, the Hardys hurried across the clearing and down a trail through the misty woods to the road. There they piled into the old jeep.

"Hang on!" said Lenny, as they started a bone-shaking ride downhill.

Twenty minutes later the car reached Main Street in Clintville and came to a stop in front of Haskins Hotel. The telephone was ringing as the boys rushed in.

Mr Haskins seized the receiver from the wall telephone. "Yep!" he shouted into the mouthpiece, then handed the instrument to Frank.

"This is Hank Shale," came a voice, barely audible

through the static. "Your pa asked me to call and say he needs your help pronto."

"Is Dad okay?" Frank asked loudly.

The answer was drowned out by crackling noises over the wire. Then the voice said, "Get here to Lucky Lode," and the line went dead.

"Hank Shale is the name of the old friend Dad told us he'd be staying with," Joe recalled. "But how do we know that was really Shale?"

"I heard the operator say it was Lucky Lode calling," put in Mr Haskins.

"That settles it then," Frank said urgently. "Something has happened. We must take off right away and help Dad!"

"There's a morning flight to the West," Joe said. "We'll *have* to make it!"

After some difficulty, the boys managed to place a call to Lucky Lode, notifying Hank of their plan to start out the next day.

"Better eat before you go," the hotel proprietor said kindly.

Gratefully the hungry boys joined Mr Haskins and Lenny at a table in the kitchen. While they ate, Frank and Joe made their plans. They asked Lenny to take them back to the cabin in his jeep and wait while they packed.

"Then we'll pick up our car at the garage, drive all night, and make Bayport by sunrise. Another car can be sent back later for the other fellows."

After the meal, the Hardys thanked Mr Haskins and hurried out with Lenny. Soon they were riding up the steep hill in the noisy jeep.

Joe shouted, "We'll have to move fast to—"

Crash! The bottom of the jeep hit a rock in the road. The vehicle lurched into the ditch and stopped against a tree.

"We can soon push it back on the road," Lenny said, as they climbed out.

"No use. We wouldn't get far, the way it's losing oil," replied Frank when he saw the extent of the damage. "We'll walk the rest of the way and you can go back for help or another car."

Lenny agreed and hurried down the hill as the Hardys began hiking up the rugged road. Their flashlights were on, but the beams hardly penetrated the thickening fog. Often they stumbled over rocks and into ruts. The night was raw and damp.

Suddenly Joe stopped. "What's that?"

For a second they both stood still and from the woods came a faint cry. "He-e-elp!"

"Come on!" Frank said tersely.

The boys cut into the woods on their right, and felt their way through the mist-shrouded trees. Low branches cut their faces, and once Joe tripped over a huge oak root.

Again they heard the thin call for help.

"Over there," said Frank, "where the fog is denser."

Cautiously they moved forward. Suddenly the cry came more loudly—from right below their feet!

"Careful," warned Frank, feeling ahead with his foot. "There's a ravine here." Half sliding, the boys worked their way down the bank. At the bottom Frank stumbled over something bulky and there came another moan. He shone his light on a prostrate figure.

"Here he is, Joe," said Frank. The two boys knelt beside the victim.

"My leg," the man groaned. "I've been shot."

With extreme care Frank pulled aside the trouser cloth torn by the bullet. "Doesn't seem to be much bleeding now, but there might be more when we move you." Quickly the boys wound their handkerchiefs loosely around the man's thigh to use as a tourniquet if necessary.

As they lifted the moaning figure, he fainted.

"No time to waste, Joe. He's pretty weak."

Joe peered around into the blanket of fog. "Suppose we can't find our cabin?" he asked grimly.

"We *must*," Frank replied. "This man may die if we don't get him to shelter."

A Suspicious Summons

TOGETHER, the boys eased the unconscious man up the bank. Then Frank hoisted him over one shoulder.

"Lucky he's not a big fellow," Joe commented.

He went ahead, beaming his light through the fog and leading Frank by one hand. Gradually the white mist grew less dense, and the Hardys could make out the shapes of trees.

"That looks like the oak where I stumbled," Joe said. "I think we go left here."

Progress was slow and uncertain. Finally Frank said, "If we don't come to the road soon, we'd better stop. We may have lost our bearings and be heading deeper into the woods."

To the boys' relief, the man's wound bled little. Just as they were about to turn back, Joe felt rocky ruts underfoot and exclaimed, "Here's the road!"

Carefully he and Frank began the climb uphill and struggled to the top. The fog had drifted and lightened in spots. The boys trudged on. Finally, Frank caught sight of the path which led to the clearing. A few minutes later the Hardys found the cabin, and Frank pounded on the door.

Biff opened it and exclaimed in amazement. Quickly

he and the other boys helped carry the man to one of the bunks and covered him. When Tony brought the oil lamp from the table, they saw that the man's face was deeply seamed by time and weather. Joe removed the man's worn woollen hat, revealing a thick thatch of grizzled hair.

While Frank cut away the victim's trouser leg and examined the bullet wound in his thigh, Joe quietly told the others all that had happened. Meantime, Biff unpacked their first-aid kit, and Chet began heating a can of soup.

"We must get this man to a doctor," Frank said as he finished bandaging the leg. "The bullet will have to be removed."

The victim groaned and his eyes fluttered open. "Wh-where am I?" he whispered.

Joe quickly explained what had happened.

"Sip this soup," Chet told the patient, "and you'll feel a lot better. I'll feed it to you."

When the stranger had finished the soup, he said in a stronger voice, "Thank you, boys, for a mighty good turn. I wish I could repay you."

"The most important thing is to get you to a doctor. We're expecting Lenny Haskins to come for—" Frank broke off as the old man gave a start. "Is anything wrong?"

"Say! Would any of you boys be Frank and Joe Hardy?" the patient inquired in a feeble voice.

The two brothers identified themselves.

"I plumb forgot, gettin' shot by that fool hunter and all," the man went on, "but you're the lads I was comin' to see. The storekeeper in Clintville said you wanted to get in touch with me."

"Are you Mike Onslow?" Frank queried.

"Yep, that's me."

"We asked about you, but the storekeeper told us you'd probably be off tending your traps," Frank went on. "He doubted we'd catch you at home, even if we could find your cabin."

Onslow nodded. "My shack's pretty hard to get to if you don't know these woods. I camp out quite a bit, anyhow, durin' the trappin' season." He gave the brothers a quizzical look. "What you want to see me about?"

"You'd better not do any more talking till you're stronger," Joe advised.

But the trapper insisted he felt equal to it, so Frank explained that their father was a private detective and had been engaged to track down a gang of criminals in Montana.

"Dad thinks they may be holed up somewhere in the country around Lucky Lode," Frank went on. "He heard out there that you had prospected the whole area about twenty-five years ago and once tangled with crooks who had a secret hideout in those parts."

Joe added, "He thought you might know of some likely spots to hunt for the gang."

The elderly trapper sighed and settled back on the bunk. His eyes took on a faraway look.

"Yep, I know the Lucky Lode country like the palm o' my hand," he murmured. "Don't reckon as I can help you much, though. But your pa's right—I did run up against a gang o' owlhoots."

"Tell us about it," Frank urged.

"Well," Onslow began, "I was partners with two brothers, John and James Coulson, and a big redheaded daredevil, Bart Dawson. We were workin' a claim in the Bitterroot Hills and we sure 'nough struck it rich."

"Gold?" Joe asked.

Onslow nodded. "Real pay dirt—we thought we were fixed for life. By the time the vein petered out, we had three bags o' nuggets and one of old gold coins we found stashed behind a rock."

"Wow! What happened?" put in Tony.

"The night we were ready to leave our claim, we were jumped by the toughest bunch o' crooks in Montana—Black Pepper and his gang. They surrounded our cabin, and we knew we'd never get away with our skins *and* the gold."

"How did you make it finally?" Chet asked.

"Well, Bart Dawson was an ex-pilot and he had an old, beat-up plane out on the plateau. We'd already put the gold aboard—easier than luggin' it on horseback. While we lured Black Pepper and his boys around to the front of the cabin, Bart slipped out back and ran for his crate. The gang spotted Bart and chased him. We heard his motor, so we knew he got away okay. Before the varmints came back, the rest of us escaped from the cabin."

"You met Dawson later?" Joe wanted to know.

Onslow's face became bitter. "We were *supposed* to meet him up in Helena and split the gold four ways. But we never saw Dawson or the gold again. Funny part of it is, Dawson was a good partner. I'd have staked my life we could trust him. But I was wrong."

"Didn't you ever hear of him afterwards, or pick up his trail?" questioned Frank.

"Nope. Never found hide nor hair o' him. After that, I got fed up prospectin'. So I come back East and settled down to scratchin' out a livin' with my traps. I lost track o' the Coulson brothers."

Everyone was silent and thoughtful for a moment. Then Joe asked Mike Onslow, "Have you any ideas as to where Dad might look for the criminals he's after?"

The woodsman chuckled dryly. "Son, there's a heap o' places he might look—awful big country out Montana way. Them mountains is full o' spots for a gang to hole up in." The trapper frowned. "One likely place was in the Lone Tree area—a box canyon part way up Windy Peak. Accordin' to rumours, that was Black Pepper's hideout."

The Hardys were excited by this information. "Thanks for the tip," said Frank. "It's tough luck, your getting shot tonight. It wouldn't have happened if you hadn't started out to see us. But maybe we can make up for it."

"Right!" Joe chimed in. "When we're out West, we'll try to find a clue to Dawson and your missing gold."

"That's kind of you, boys," said the trapper, "but I don't think there's much use. If Dawson really stole that gold, there wouldn't be much left after twenty-five years. All the same," he added spunkily, "if you're willin' to try, I'll help you if I can."

Onslow scratched his head and was thoughtful for a moment. "Don't know if it'll do any good, but I'll draw you a map of our claim."

"That'll be a starting point, anyhow," Frank said.

While the boys packed the Hardys' gear, Onslow drew a map for Frank and Joe. "Here's where the claim was," he said, marking an X. "This region was called the Lone Tree area because of a giant pine which stood all by itself on a cliff. Everybody out there knows Lone Tree," he added.

As Joe tucked the map into his pocket, someone pounded on the door. It was Lenny. "Are you ready?" he asked, panting. "The jeep's fixed."

Frank told him about finding Onslow with the gunshot wound. Then the boys improvised a stretcher, and Frank and Joe carried the injured trapper out to the jeep. While they were placing him on the back seat, Tony, Chet, and Biff collected and stowed the Hardys' gear. A few moments later Lenny started the engine and they took off.

"So long!" Frank and Joe called from the jeep.

"Good luck!" chorused Chet and the others.

When Lenny reached town, he drove straight to the local doctor's surgery. Despite their hurry, the Hardys waited to hear Dr Knapp's report after the bullet had been removed.

"He'll have to stay off that leg and have nursing care," Dr Knapp advised as he washed his hands. "He ought to go to the hospital."

"I have no money for that," Mike spoke up. "I'll look after myself."

"No, you won't," Frank said with a smile. "We'll take you back to Bayport with us."

"You bet!" his brother added. "Mother and Aunt Gertrude will like having somebody to fuss over."

The injured man protested that he did not want to be a nuisance, but the boys won their point. After picking up their car at the garage, they drove all night and arrived in Bayport at dawn. Quietly they carried Onslow up to their room. Then Frank awakened his mother and explained what had happened. She smiled understandingly and soon she and Mr Hardy's sister, Gertrude, were welcoming the woodsman warmly.

"You look as though you're in need of a good meal," Miss Hardy stated. She was a tall, spare woman with a tart tongue but a warm heart.

"We'll fix something right now," agreed the boys' slim, attractive mother.

As Frank and Joe hurried downstairs after the women Aunt Gertrude clucked disapprovingly. "Flying around in airplanes, traipsing about the Wild West chasing outlaws! You boys are headed for trouble again."

"We hope so, Aunty." Joe laughed as his aunt sniffed and bustled into the kitchen with Mrs Hardy.

Frank called the airport to check on their plane time and reported to Joe. "We have one hour to shower, dress, drive to the airport, and buy our tickets."

"We can take our camping gear just as it is," said his brother.

The boys wasted no time getting ready, and soon were on their way. They pulled up in the car park outside the air terminal with ten minutes to spare. Frank paid for their tickets and booked the baggage through to Cold Springs, the closest airport to Lucky Lode. Meantime, Joe wired their father.

As the brothers sank into their plane seats, Joe exclaimed with a grin, "We made it!"

"But we have to change at Chicago and Butte," Frank reminded him.

As soon as the plane was airborne, a hot breakfast was served. After eating, the boys took a nap for a couple of hours. When they awoke, Joe took out the map Onslow had drawn.

"It shows the area around the claim," he remarked, studying it closely. "But not how to get there from Lucky Lode."

Joe was replacing the sketch in his wallet, when the pilot's voice announced that they were coming into Chicago's O'Hare Airport. After disembarking, Frank and Joe checked at the airline ticket counter. A clerk told them that the plane they were to board would be three hours late in taking off.

Just then a quiet voice behind them asked, "Are you the Hardy boys?"

The brothers turned to face the speaker—a well-dressed man in dark clothes. "Yes, we are," Frank replied.

"My name is Hopkins," the stranger said. "I've had word from your father that I'm to give you some important reports. Unfortunately, I didn't have time to stop by my office to get them, so I'll have to ask you to come there with me."

Frank looked at Joe. They had never heard the detective mention Mr Hopkins. The man smiled. "I'm glad to see you're cautious," he said. "But I assure you this is on the level. Your father called me this morning."

The boys realized they did not know all Mr Hardy's associates. It *was* possible the man was telling the truth. Both Frank and Joe reasoned that Hank Shale could have mentioned Mr Hopkins over the telephone, but they had missed it because the connection had been so bad.

"Whom is Dad staying with?" Frank asked as a test.

"Hank Shale," Mr Hopkins replied promptly. Then he added seriously, "The reports are very important, boys." Frank and Joe knew they would have to risk accompanying him.

"All right," Frank said. "Let's go."

"My car and chauffeur are right outside," Mr Hopkins told them, walking towards the door.

The brothers followed him to a large black saloon parked at the kerb. The chauffeur opened the rear door. The boys climbed in. Mr Hopkins seated himself in front.

Suddenly, as the driver started the motor, both rear doors opened and two big, tough-looking men slid in, one on each side of the Hardys.

Instantly Frank and Joe realized this was a trap. Joe reached across to the dashboard in a desperate effort to switch off the engine. The two thugs pushed him back roughly.

"None o' that!" one snarled as the car shot away from the kerb. "From here on you kids'll take orders from us. Don't argue or we'll shut you up in a way you won't like!"

·3·

Shortcut to Peril

FRANK and Joe gritted their teeth, furious at having walked into a trap. The two thugs kept an iron grip on the boys.

"Where are you guys taking us?" Joe asked angrily.

Hopkins turned around in the front seat and gave a nasty sneer. "You're both going on a little trip. You'll soon find out where." He added gloatingly, "We knew that you'd show up at the airport today."

He now addressed one henchman, a flashily dressed fellow. "Robby, gag these kids if they squawk. And you, Zeke, let them see what you'll use on them if you have to."

Zeke, who was wearing a brown suit and shirt, opened his huge hand and revealed a small blackjack. Without a word he gave the boys a threatening look and closed his hand again.

The car moved smoothly through traffic and the boys' captors never loosened their grasp. After a long drive, the car reached a wide avenue in one of the Chicago suburbs. Slowing down, it turned into a side street and pulled into the driveway of a very old house near the corner. The driver parked at the back and the four men hustled the Hardys inside. They went upstairs to an open hallway protected by a railing.

"Get in there!" Zeke ordered, and pushed the boys

into a room near the head of the stairs. There was one window with the curtains drawn and a table.

"What's this all about?" Frank demanded.

Hopkins ignored the question. "Empty your pockets!" he barked.

Zeke opened his hand, disclosing the blackjack. Realizing that resistance was pointless, the brothers obeyed.

"You won't need this stuff," Hopkins said, as tickets, money, and keys were laid on the table.

Going through Joe's wallet, Hopkins found the map which Mike Onslow had drawn. Hopkins gave the boys a hard look. "Where did you get this?"

"What do you want with us?" Frank countered.

Hopkins' eyes glittered menacingly. "So you won't talk about the map. Well, you will later." He folded the map and put it into his pocket. "The boss'll be interested to hear about this," he said to his companions. "Now tie up these smart alecks."

With a sneer the driver of the car pulled several lengths of heavy cord from his pocket. Robby bound the Hardys' wrists behind their backs, while Zeke began tying their ankles together.

As his henchmen finished, Hopkins snapped, "I have to get downtown. Nick, go out and start the car." When the chauffeur left, Hopkins said to Zeke and Robby, "Don't forget—I'll need one of you a little later."

"How about me?" Robby asked hopefully.

"You'll do." Hopkins glanced at his wristwatch. "There'll be a taxi here to pick you up at noon— twenty-three minutes from now. Be ready."

As Hopkins moved towards the door, Joe asked hotly,

"How long are you going to keep us here?"

"Until your father drops the case he's on."

After a short interval there came the sound of a car driving away. Within seconds Zeke said to Robby, "Let's go downstairs and eat some lunch."

"And leave these boys?" Robby asked. "Zeke, you're crazy. They might get loose."

A crafty look came into Zeke's eyes as he gazed at a wardrobe. It had an old-fashioned wooden latch.

"We'll lock 'em in there," he said. "If they try to bust out, we'll hear 'em and come runnin'."

"Okay," Robby agreed. "And for safety we'll lock the hall door."

Frank and Joe were dragged into the wardrobe and the latch was secured. The men left the room. At once the Hardys began trying to free themselves. Frank managed to back close to his brother, and with his fingers, work at Joe's wrist bonds.

"We sure made a blunder," Frank said grimly. "Dad told us before he left that the gang he's after is widespread."

"What puzzles me," Joe replied, as he finally extricated his hands from the loosened ropes, and untied Frank's wrist cords, "is how they knew we were heading for the West?"

Frank shrugged as he and Joe freed their ankles. "We'll find out later. Right now we must escape."

Joe was already feeling around the wardrobe. On a hook hung a slender metal coat hanger. "I'll try this," he said. "The door crack by the latch is pretty wide. Hurray! The hanger goes through!"

It was only a matter of moments before the wooden

latch had been pushed upward, and the boys stepped out of the wardrobe. They pocketed the tickets, money, and wallets, which were still on the table.

Joe whispered, "The hall door won't be so easy."

Frank had tiptoed to the one window in the room. He pushed aside the curtains and looked down on to a shabby yard.

"Too far to drop down there," he muttered. "We'll just have to rush those men when they come back."

The next instant came the sound of heavy footsteps pounding up the stairs. Joe stepped to one side of the door while Frank crouched in the centre of the room.

The key turned in the lock and the door burst open. Frank charged forward, butting Zeke squarely in the stomach. The blow sent the man reeling across the hall against the railing. Zeke toppled over it backwards with a shriek of panic and would have plunged to the floor below had he not grabbed one of the rails.

Enraged, Zeke's partner seized Frank by the shoulder and swung him around for a punch. Joe rushed out through the doorway. His fist landed hard on the back of Robby's skull and the man collapsed in a heap.

"Come on! Let's go!" Frank exclaimed.

Zeke snarled and tried desperately to pull himself back up over the railing as the two boys dashed downstairs and out the front door. To their relief, they saw a taxi waiting at the curb, its motor idling.

"Boy! We timed things just right!" Joe exclaimed gleefully.

The driver, a thin-faced, hawk-nosed man, looked at the boys in surprise as they yanked open the car door and climbed in.

"O'Hare Airport," Frank ordered. "Fast as you can make it!"

The driver threw the car into gear and pulled away from the kerb. Frank and Joe looked back at the house. As the taxi reached the corner and swung on to the avenue, the boys caught a glimpse of Robby rushing from the house.

"I'll bet he's mad enough to chew nails!" Joe thought with a chuckle.

"I'd like to see Hopkins' face when Robby reports what happened," Frank whispered.

"Can't you go any faster?" Joe asked the driver. "We have to catch a plane."

The taxi driver glanced at the Hardys in his mirror. "Sure. I'll take a shortcut."

He turned right at the next corner. After threading his way through several narrow side streets, the driver came to another avenue. Here he swung right again.

The Hardys were puzzled. Although the side streets had slanted and twisted somewhat, it seemed as if they were now heading back in the same direction from which they had come! Joe was about to protest when Frank clutched his arm.

He pointed furtively to the taxi driver's identification card. The photograph on the card showed a chubby man with a small button nose. He looked nothing like the hawk-featured driver.

Joe gulped as he realized that this driver was an impostor—most likely one of Hopkins' thugs! The boys had escaped from Zeke and Robby only to fall straight into the clutches of another member of the gang!

· 4 ·

A Painted Warning

THE Hardys looked at each other, speechless. No
wonder the taxi driver had seemed surprised! He must
have guessed they had escaped from Zeke and Robby.
But he had not dared risk any strong-arm tactics in full
view of the neighbouring houses.

Probably, Frank thought, he had driven around to
gain time while figuring out his next move. Maybe the
driver, too, had glimpsed Robby and was circling back
to the house for help.

Joe wondered, "Could we tackle him without
causing an accident? I'm afraid not."

As if reading his brother's mind, Frank scribbled a
note on his plane-ticket envelope:

Hop out at first red light!

Joe nodded tensely. Two blocks later traffic lights
loomed. They were just changing to yellow. The driver
tried to beat the lights, but an oncoming car made a
left turn, blocking his way, and he had to slam on the
brakes. Frank nudged his brother towards the right-
hand door and Joe jerked it open.

"Hey! What's the idea?" the driver snarled as the
boys leaped out. "Come back!"

30

Frank and Joe sprinted across the street. Reaching the kerb, they glanced back. The driver was still snarling at them, but they could not hear what he was saying. Then the lights changed and he was forced to move on in the surge of traffic.

"He may try a U-turn!" Frank said. "Let's go!"

"Wait! Here comes another taxi!" Joe exclaimed. They flagged it down and jumped in. "O'Hare Airport! Step on it!" Frank ordered.

As the taxi sped off, the boys watched out of the rear window. But no one was in pursuit.

"Whew!" Joe said, giving a sigh of relief. "Good thing you spotted that identification photo!"

Frank nodded. "That thug must have stolen the car from the real driver—and not just to trap us," he whispered. "I'll bet it was to be used for pulling another job!"

"Right! That's why Hopkins told Robby exactly when it would arrive—they may be planning a carefully timed holdup!"

It was only a few minutes before take-off when the boys dashed into the air terminal. Frank made a hasty call to Captain Jaworski of the Chicago Police, an old friend. Frank quickly explained what had happened and told the chief their theory that the gang might be planning to use the stolen taxi for some crooked job.

"The name on the real driver's identification card was Ira Kleeder," Frank added.

"Good enough. We can get the licence number from the taxi company. And thanks for the tip!"

Joe, who was standing watch outside the telephone booth, rapped on the glass and pointed frantically to his wristwatch. Frank rang off, and the boys raced to the loading gate.

"We nearly left without you," the stewardess said as she welcomed them aboard the plane. The Hardys smiled and found seats.

Soon they were airborne. The two boys settled back as the plane headed west.

"I'd sure like to know how Hopkins got word we were on our way to Lucky Lode," Frank mused.

"The gang out there must have informed him," Joe said. "Remember—he even knows that Dad is staying with Hank Shale."

"Another thing," Frank went on, "why should they be interested in that map? Is there some connection between Onslow's claim and the gang? We'd better ask Mike to send us another map."

"I can remember it pretty clearly," Joe assured him, then added soberly, "Why didn't Dad call us himself? I hope he's not hurt."

Frank nodded, troubled. Lunch was served aboard the plane. Afterwards, the boys dozed.

At Butte they were wary, staying close to other passengers as they changed planes. No one bothered them, however. Soon they were winging their way in a twin-engined craft over the frozen ridges of the Rockies towards Cold Springs, the small airport serving Lucky Lode.

The plane set down bumpily on a snow-covered landing strip. As the Hardys came out and gazed around, a sharp, biting wind hit their faces.

"Wow! This sure is different!" said Frank.

Pine woods surrounded the bleak, windswept field

with its small terminal and hangar. A helicopter
and a tiny single-engine aircraft were parked near the
edge of the field. To the west loomed the snowy
Bitterroot mountain range.

"*Brr!*" Joe shivered. "Lonely looking, eh?"

"Sure is." Frank replied.

As the brothers headed for the terminal, a hatless
man in a plaid mackinaw strode towards them. "Frank
and Joe Hardy?" he boomed.

He was a tall, handsome, ruddy-faced man. His
white hair blew about in the wind. "I'm Bob Dodge,"
he added, shaking hands with the boys heartily. "Your
father's working on a case for me in Lucky Lode. I
came over in my helicopter to pick you up."

"Why didn't Dad come?" Frank asked.

"He had an accident—broke a couple of ribs.
Nothing serious," Dodge added, "but the doctor taped
his chest and wants him to keep quiet."

Seeing a look of suspicion on the boys' faces, Dodge
took a picture from his pocket. "Your father gave me
this." He held out a snapshot of the Hardys' house with
Aunt Gertrude standing on the lawn. "That's your
father's sister," Dodge said.

"Okay." Frank knew that if the detective had been
forced to hand over the picture, he would not have
given Aunt Gertrude's true identity. Mr Dodge must
be all right.

"We have to be careful," Joe explained.

"I understand." Dodge smiled. "There's some stuff
in the terminal I want to pick up. You two go on
aboard." He gestured towards the helicopter.

The boys started across the field. They were still

some distance from the craft when a tall, thin man suddenly jumped out of the helicopter and walked rapidly away.

"Wonder who he is?" Joe asked.

"Maybe an airport attendant," Frank guessed.

"If so, why is he heading for the woods?"

Frank frowned. When they reached the helicopter, he said, "I wish we knew what that fellow was doing aboard."

Joe pulled back the door and looked inside cautiously. The boys searched the helicopter but found nothing.

Frank chuckled in relief. "Okay, we didn't get booby-trapped. Let's stow our gear."

They climbed out and Joe was about to open the access hatch to the baggage compartment, just aft of the cabin, when Frank stopped him.

"Let's play safe and check this door."

"Good idea." Frank took a rope from his gear and tied one end to the hatch handle. The boys backed off to one side. Frank tugged the rope.

Boo-o-om! A deafening blast rocked the craft and knocked the boys off their feet. An acrid smell of gunpowder assailed their nostrils.

"Good grief!" Joe whispered.

Pale and shaken, they examined the baggage compartment. A sawed-off shotgun had been wired and propped into position inside, evidently by someone working through a removable panel in the forward wall. The gun had been triggered by a cord tied to the door latch.

Meanwhile, the explosion had brought Bob Dodge

and an older man running from the terminal. "What happened?" they yelled together.

Frank explained, and the two men examined the deadly set up with dismayed looks. Joe cautioned them not to touch the weapon so it could be checked for fingerprints. Dodge's companion, who proved to be the airport manager, went off to report the incident to the police.

Frank and Joe took out their fingerprint kit and dusted the shotgun. No prints appeared.

"The man we saw at the 'copter wore gloves," Frank recalled, "but I was hoping something might show up, anyhow."

"The gun must have been wiped clean beforehand," Joe deduced.

Soon two police officers arrived. The Hardys described their near-fatal experience, and reported the results of their fingerprint check.

"You're detectives?" one officer asked.

Frank introduced himself and his brother as Fenton Hardy's sons. "I see," said the officer. "I've heard of him—rarely fails to solve a case. So you're following in his footsteps. Well, good luck!"

The brothers turned over the weapon to the policemen, who then, with the boys assisting, made a thorough check of the helicopter. They found no clues, however, so the Hardys stowed their gear and followed Dodge aboard the whirlybird.

"That scattergun could have been meant for me," Dodge remarked worriedly, as he started the motor.

"Or for us," Frank said.

As the helicopter rose and soared towards the

Bitterroot mountain range, Frank told Dodge of their being kidnapped in Chicago.

"What is the case Dad is working on for you?" Joe asked.

"I've been running an armoured-car service for ten years," the big man explained. "Recently one of my trucks was hijacked and a money shipment stolen. Both guards aboard were shot. The money was insured, of course, but I wanted those hijackers caught to avoid any future holdups, so, knowing your father's reputation for tracking down hijackers, I engaged him to investigate. My men's safety is important to me. The police have worked on the case, too. They and your father managed to recover the money and catch two of the gang, but the others escaped. Someone reported seeing them in Canada."

"Then why has Dad stayed here?" Frank asked.

"Because he believes the leader of the gang, Big Al Martin, is still in this area. Your father refuses to leave until he is found."

"How did Dad get hurt?" Joe questioned.

"He was thrown from a horse yesterday afternoon," Dodge replied, "while chasing a fellow he thinks is one of Big Al's men."

"And now Dad wants us to try to find the outlaws," Frank surmised.

"Yes," Dodge said, "and the sooner the better. Big Al's dangerous—he belongs behind bars. The police know he has henchmen in other cities."

As Dodge spoke, the helicopter shook and rattled in the wind. Below them, the boys saw wild, rugged country. Snow-covered buttes stood like gaunt sentinels overlooking heavily wooded valleys.

Presently Dodge shouted, "It won't be long now!"

Ahead, in a mountain cleft, the pilot pointed out the tiny town of Lucky Lode. "Over to the left is Windy Peak—the highest in the range."

"Have you been flying long, Mr Dodge?" Joe asked.

"I started taking lessons a couple of years ago and it came easily to me."

"Have you always lived in the West?" Frank asked, but Dodge did not reply.

"Here we go!" he said, and began setting the helicopter down. Frank wondered if Dodge had not heard his question or did not want to discuss his past.

The pilot landed expertly in a clearing at one end of Lucky Lode. Then he helped the boys lug their gear to Hank Shale's cabin at the foot of a steep hill on the outskirts of the town.

When Frank knocked, the door was opened by a tall, skinny man with thinning red hair. His wrinkled face split into a grin when he saw the trio.

"Come in and thaw out!" he exclaimed. "I'm Hank Shale. Your pa and I've been waitin' for you!"

The boys entered to find their father seated before a roaring fire. Fenton Hardy was a trim, athletic-looking man. His keen eyes lit up when he saw his sons.

"Hello, boys," said the detective, and moving carefully, shook hands with them. "Thanks for giving up your camping trip."

"We'd rather work with you any day," Joe said, grinning.

Mr Hardy smiled and turned to Dodge. "I appreciate your bringing my sons."

Hank announced that he was going to the kitchen to rustle up some grub.

"I'll help you," Dodge volunteered. "The three detectives can sit by the fire and exchange news."

In low voices the boys told their father all that had happened since they had left Bayport.

Mr Hardy looked grave. "I agree with you that someone here must have informed Al's Chicago henchmen that you were coming. But who?" He glanced towards the kitchen and called, "Hank!"

When the red-haired man appeared in the doorway, Mr Hardy asked him, "Who was in Burke's general store when you phoned my sons last night?"

"Just the usual crowd o' fellers sittin' around the stove," Hank replied. "I had to holler on account o' that bad connection, so they all heard every word."

"Someone on the line might have been listening, too," Joe remarked.

"I smell somethin' burnin'!" Hank exclaimed and bolted into the kitchen.

"We'll have to be on guard," said Frank. "Someone probably will be watching every move we make."

"Dad," Joe asked, "what made you so sure Big Al didn't go to Canada?"

"I was working with the police," Mr Hardy said, "when we caught two of the gang the week before last. One of them told us Big Al *was* hiding out here, and meant to attend to some unfinished business. The police thought he was lying in order to sidetrack us while Al made an escape. I had a hunch it was the truth."

"Why?" asked Frank.

"Because the man seemed scared and appeared to be

hoping for a break at his trial. I started riding the hills trying to pick up Al's trail. Yesterday I followed a rough-looking fellow on horseback. He met another man in a small clearing. I heard them talking and caught the words 'Big Al' and 'hideout'. Just then my horse, Major, whinnied and the men galloped off. I gave chase, but Major stumbled and I took a spill." The detective smiled ruefully. "Now I'm stuck here! Boys," he added seriously, "your job is to find that hideout."

Frank and Joe, greatly excited by this challenge, discussed it all during a supper of thick western steaks, beans, and bread.

"We'll have to get a line on what Big Al's unfinished business is," Frank said, when they were seated around the fireplace later.

"In any event, it's probably illegal," his father rejoined.

Presently Dodge got up. "Guess I'd better get back to the hotel."

"Are your offices in Lucky Lode?" Joe asked.

"No, in Helena. I've been staying in town to watch developments on the case. If there's any way I can help you, boys," the big man added, "just let me know."

After Dodge had left, Mr Hardy remarked, "Bob strikes me as a fine man. Never mentions his early days, but I'm told he started his business on a shoestring and built it up by hard work."

"Speakin' o' work, who wants to wash dishes?"

Laughing, the boys took Hank's hint and before long the kitchen was shipshape.

Finally the brothers went to bed in one of two small

rooms which led off the big one. Weary, the boys fell asleep immediately.

Suddenly they awoke with a start. A rumbling noise was coming from behind the cabin, growing louder every moment. The brothers leaped from bed. At the same instant, the cabin was jarred with a deafening crash.

Frank and Joe heard Hank yell as they rushed into the living-room. "Look! Fire!" He pointed to the kitchen where a bright red glow was visible.

The trio dashed in. By the light of the flames they could see that a huge boulder had crashed through the back wall, overturning the stove and spewing burning firewood over the floor.

The boys raced back to their bedroom to get blankets. Spreading them over the fire, they began smothering and stamping out the flames. Mr Hardy had hurried from his room, but the boys would not allow him to help. Meanwhile, Hank had filled a bucket at the kitchen pump and was dousing water over the hot stove. The fire sizzled angrily but gradually died out.

"Tarnation!" Hank exclaimed. "Nearest thing to an avalanche we've ever had around here." He lighted an oil lamp, and everyone surveyed the damage.

"What a mess!" Joe grimaced.

The cabin owner sighed. "A whoppin' big hole in the wall, and some burnt floorin'. Well, I reckon I can fix it tomorrow."

Frank and Joe started to push the boulder out through the hole, then Joe gasped in surprise. On the huge stone were brightly painted red letters. Rolling the boulder a bit farther, the boys made out a crudely painted message:

HARDYS—LEAVE TOWN!

"A warning from Big Al!" Frank said grimly.

· 5 ·

The Strange Blue Light

THE three detectives and Hank examined the warning message on the huge rock.

"Big Al is a rough customer," Mr Hardy said, frowning. "Be on your guard at all times."

"We'll watch out, Dad," Frank promised.

He and Joe shoved the boulder outside and looked up the hill. The moon had set and the mountainside was shrouded in darkness.

"No telling if anyone's up there," Joe muttered.

The two brothers shivered in the icy wind, and then squirmed through the hole into the burned kitchen. Meanwhile, Hank pulled on warm clothes, went out to a lean-to, and brought back a tarpaulin. The boys helped him nail it over the hole in the wall, then set the stove up.

"That'll do till mornin'," Hank said.

Frank and Joe were up as soon as it was light. After a quick breakfast they climbed the steep, snow-covered slope behind the shack, following the trail ploughed by the huge boulder. The boys soon found a deep gouge where the stone had been pried out of the hillside.

"Somebody used a crowbar to get it going," Joe said, kneeling on the ground.

"And here are some traces of red paint," Frank pointed out.

They scouted around thoroughly, and noticed the snow had been disturbed, as if to cover tracks.

"Whoever pried that stone loose," Frank said thoughtfully, "may have come from town rather than from a hideout in the hills."

"Why?"

"Because it's not likely that anyone hiding up in the mountains would have red paint on hand. The person who did this probably got it at the village store."

The boys walked on up the hill. The undergrowth at the top was parted and broken.

"Someone forced his way through here," Frank said.

They followed the tramped brush to a trail which led along the wooded ridge, paralleling the main street of Lucky Lode below them. Soon they spotted a narrow path leading down into the small community.

"The man we're after could have come this way," Frank said. "We'd better scout for clues."

Slowly he and Joe walked down the steep, narrow trail. There were footprints, but these were too jumbled to be of any significance. They reached the bottom without finding anything else, then climbed back to the top and continued along the ridge.

After a while the boys emerged into a clearing. Before them lay an old cemetery. They crawled through a gap in the dilapidated wooden fence and walked silently among the gravestones. From the bleak, windswept spot they could see all of Lucky Lode in the valley below. The old part of town ended directly under the cemetery.

"Look at these, Frank," called Joe, from where he knelt beside a double headstone.

" 'John and James Coulson'!" Frank read. "Mike Onslow's partners!"

"I guess they came to Lucky Lode to try for another stake," Joe said.

"You're probably right," Frank replied.

The boys decided to go into town and headed for the cemetery gate. Coarse brush grew up around the ornate posts. Frank passed through, but Joe was pulled up short.

"Wait!" he said. "I'm caught!"

Big burrs clung to his trousers. Fumbling with heavily gloved fingers, he managed to get free. Together, he and Frank pulled out all the burrs and the brothers scrambled down the slope.

At the foot they saw the deserted grey-weathered buildings. As they walked along the old wooden sidewalk, the boards creaked and the wind rattled the loose doors and shutters.

"This end of Lucky Lode's a real ghost town," Frank remarked.

"Somebody lives here, though," Joe replied. He pointed ahead to a tumbledown house. A pale stream of smoke issued from the chimney.

Suddenly the door opened a crack and a rifle muzzle poked out. It was aimed straight at the boys!

Frank and Joe halted, not knowing whether to drop to the ground or run. But nothing happened. At last they moved forward cautiously.

The muzzle followed the Hardys until they came abreast of the porch. Then the door was kicked open and an old man jumped out, aiming the weapon at them. Frank and Joe stopped.

"What are you doin' here?" the white-haired man demanded curtly, his eyes squinting suspiciously.

"Just visiting," Frank said in a friendly tone.

"We're from the East," Joe went on. "Staying with Hank Shale."

The old man lowered the rifle. "Oh," he said, relieved. "Any friend of Hank Shale is a friend of mine. Come on in."

"Did you expect somebody else?" Frank asked, as the boys followed the old man into the shack.

"Don't know!" he snapped. "A fella can't be too careful around here now. There's funny things happenin' up on Cemetery Hill."

The boys found themselves in a plainly furnished room heated by a wood stove. They introduced themselves and their host said, "My name's Ben Tinker." He pointed to two wooden chairs near the stove. "Sit down and warm up."

"What did you mean by funny things going on in the cemetery?" Frank asked him.

"It's haunted," Ben said flatly. "Has been for the past two weeks."

"Haunted!" Joe echoed. "How?"

"Sometimes, late at night, a blue light blinks on and off up there. I've seen it," the old man explained, "because I'm a night owl and like a breath of air before turnin' in."

"Has anyone else seen the light?" Frank asked.

"Doubt it. In Lucky Lode nobody's out late at night. But that's not all," Ben went on. "About an hour after the lights show, somebody walks past here. I think it's Charlie's ghost. Charlie used to play piano in the Peacock Dance Hall next door. He was killed in a gunfight there forty years ago and buried up on Cemetery Hill."

The Hardys were mystified. "Why do you think it's Charlie's ghost, Ben?" Frank asked.

"Because some nights I hear the piano—it's still there. Sort of tuneless, like when Charlie let his fingers wander over the keys."

"When was the last time you saw the blue light?" Frank queried.

"Night before last."

"You don't really believe it's a ghost, do you?" Joe said.

"Might be. Then again might not. Somebody might be up to monkey business," Ben admitted. "That's why I keep this handy." He pointed to the rifle leaning against the wall.

Frank, on impulse, asked the old-timer, "Do you know anything about John and James Coulson?"

"Sure do. They died in a mining accident about twenty-five years ago, after some varmints stole a lot o' gold from them."

"We'd like to hear the story," Frank said quickly.

Ben's rambling account of the Lone Tree incident agreed with the version the Hardys had heard from Mike Onslow.

"What happened to Bart Dawson?" Joe asked.

"Can't say for sure," was Ben's reply, "but he must have kept the gold. I saw him in Helena a couple o' years after and he acted like he didn't know me. Why would he have done that if he hadn't been guilty?"

The Hardys exchanged glances. It certainly sounded as though Mike Onslow's ex-partner had absconded with the gold! The brothers got up to leave, and Frank said, "Thanks for telling us all this, Ben."

"Any time, boys. Come back again," the man urged. "But stay away from that graveyard!"

As the Hardys walked down the main street towards the populated part of Lucky Lode, Frank suggested that the blue light could be a signal.

"I think so, too," Joe agreed. "Cemetery Hill is clearly visible from everywhere in town."

"It would be an ideal place for Big Al to signal a spy if he had one in Lucky Lode," Frank remarked.

"Ben said the light has been around for only a couple of weeks," Joe added, "and that's about the length of time Dad thinks Big Al has been hiding out near here."

"The footsteps Ben hears could be the spy returning to town after meeting Al in the cemetery," Frank speculated.

"What about the piano playing in the deserted dance hall?" Joe asked.

"Maybe it's Ben Tinker's imagination."

By this time the boys had reached the business section of Main Street. Frank stopped in front of the general store. "Let's go in and see if we can find out anything about that red paint."

Inside, a husky man stood behind the counter, slitting open boxes with his pocketknife. Frank asked if he were the owner.

"I am," he said. "Jim Burke's the name."

Frank and Joe told him who they were, and he introduced the boys to several men seated around a potbelly stove. The Hardys noticed that the town post office, telephone switchboard, and telegraph office were also in the store.

"You must know everything that's going on in town, Mr Burke," Joe said, smiling.

"That's right," the man answered with a wink.

"Could you tell us which stores here stock red paint?" Frank asked.

Burke chuckled. "This is the only store there is," he replied. "I stock it. You want some?"

"No," said Joe. "We'd like to find out if anyone bought red paint in the past few weeks."

"No one," Burke told him promptly. "I'd remember because I don't sell much of it. Why?"

While Frank described the boulder attack on Hank's cabin, he and Joe watched their listeners' faces. None showed any sign of guilt. The Hardys told about meeting Ben Tinker and asked if anyone else had seen the blue light at the top of Cemetery Hill.

Burke laughed. "Ben Tinker's always imaginin' things."

One of the other men guffawed. "A couple of weeks ago he was seein' men from outer space."

The Hardys did not believe this but made no comment. They left the store and went back to their cabin. Here they found Hank Shale and their father repairing the damaged wall.

"You'd better take it easy, Dad," Joe said with concern.

"Oh, I haven't been exerting myself." Fenton Hardy

grinned at his sons. "I have to find *some* way to work off a little energy."

While Hank fixed lunch, Frank and Joe related what they had found out.

"Ben *is* an old man," Hank put in as he dished out a sizzling plateful of ham and eggs, "but he's not loco. Still, the whole story, blue lights and all, might be just his imagination."

That afternoon the boys insisted that their father remain quiet while they helped Hank rebuild the cabin wall. By nightfall the job was done.

While they were relaxing in front of the fire after supper, Hank told the boys where they could rent horses to search for Big Al's hideout. "I only have my old mare Daisy," he added, "and she's none too spry."

"There are a number of abandoned mines in this area," Mr Hardy told his sons. "I suggest you investigate them."

"But watch out for tommy-knockers," Hank warned with a grin.

"Tommy-knockers? What're they?" Joe asked.

"Some kind o' gnomes or spirits or suchlike that live underground. Old-time miners used to say that if you heard one knockin', it meant there was about to be an accident."

"Okay. If we hear any, we'll watch our step," Frank promised jokingly. "By the way, we'd like to search the Lone Tree area. Where was Mike Onslow's claim located?"

"Nobody knows, any more," Hank said, scratching his head. "The Lone Tree territory's too big for you fellows to cover alone."

He drew them a sketch, showing the location of Lone Tree and deserted mines in the area. Frank and Joe decided which ones they would try next day.

Later, the brothers walked down to the livery stable on Main Street and rented horses for their expedition. The boys rode back to the cabin and stabled the animals in Hank's lean-to. When they returned, Hank and Mr Hardy were asleep, but the boys sat up for a while and discussed the mystery. They became aware that the wind had risen and was whipping around the cabin.

"We'd better take a look at the horses," Frank suggested.

Bundling into their heavy jackets, the boys went outside. The lean-to was snugly built and the animals seemed comfortable. Satisfied, Frank and Joe started back. As they rounded the corner of Hank's cabin, they stopped short.

"Look!" breathed Joe.

Clearly visible on the top of Cemetery Hill was a winking blue light!

·6·

Ghost Music

"LET'S go up there!" urged Frank, grabbing Joe's arm.

As quickly and quietly as possible, the boys scaled the hill at the back of Hank's cabin and hurried along the ridge trail towards the graveyard. When they reached the edge of the clearing, Frank and Joe paused in the shelter of the trees.

The night was moonless but the northern lights made great coloured streaks across the sky. In a back corner of the cemetery, the brothers spotted a tall, thin figure.

"Probably the person who signalled with the blue light!" Joe whispered.

Crouching low, the young detectives crept through the broken fence. They moved forward soundlessly to a large stone monument and knelt behind it. The Hardys wished they could get closer to the man, but that gravestone was the only one large enough to afford them cover.

The man paced about restlessly, stamping his feet and hunching his shoulders for warmth. Presently the boys heard the sound of footsteps in the front of the cemetery. A second figure, big and bulky, approached the first. The newcomer's cap was pulled low, and his face appeared to be muffled for protection against the bitter cold. He took up a position with his back turned to the two brothers.

As the thin man spoke, Frank and Joe strained their ears to hear above the roaring of the wind. They were able to catch only a part of the conversation.

". . . Big Al's plenty mad," the first man was saying. "He gave me special orders for you tonight, Slip Gun."

The big man was silent, apparently waiting for the speaker to continue.

"He wants you to keep the Hardy boys bottled up in town," the thin man went on. "Also, be sure to tip him off on every move they make."

The other man's muffled response was drowned by the wind. Evidently he had asked a question.

"No luck yet," the tall figure declared. "He'd better forget . . . that special business . . . it's hopeless . . . meeting day after tomorrow . . . wants . . . the usual stuff."

"Where?"

"Shadow of the Bear," answered the thin man.

The next instant there came the loud crack of breaking twigs. Both men whirled towards the noise. The boys held their breath. Was somebody else in the graveyard?

After a long silence, the thin man said, "Tomorrow Jake and I . . . with the boss . . . Brady's Mine. It's one that ain't flooded."

Frank's and Joe's hearts jumped with excitement, but the wind rose to a howl and they could hear no more. The men murmured together for a few minutes, then parted.

The thin man moved past the Hardys' hiding place.

He slipped through the gap in the fence and quickly disappeared into the woods. Soon afterwards, the boys heard a horse whinny and a brief clatter of hoofs on rocky ground.

"No chance of following *him*," Joe muttered. "He might have led us to the gang's hideout, too."

Just then the other man trudged by. The boys waited tensely until the bulky figure reached the gate.

"Joe," whispered Frank, "we can still find out who Big Al's spy in town is."

Cautiously the boys started towards the cemetery gate. They could hear the big man ahead, slipping and slithering along over the stony, snow-covered hill. The Hardys followed him as closely as they dared, moving furtively from one patch of scrub brush to another.

Suddenly Frank stopped short to listen. He thought he had heard a noise behind them and seized his brother's arm to alert him. Startled, Joe slipped and nearly fell. A shower of stones cascaded down the hill!

There was silence on the dark slope. Frank and Joe stood motionless, listening intently. They could imagine the burly figure ahead listening as well. Then, from behind them, another rock came tumbling down.

Joe nudged Frank. "We didn't cause that! Someone's following us!"

Had the thin man spotted them, the Hardys wondered, and doubled back to stalk them? Or had a third person been in the cemetery, as they suspected?

The brothers scanned the hill above, but could see no one. "He's probably hiding behind boulders or scrub," Frank whispered.

After a while the Hardys thought they detected

sounds of movement below them. Warily they descended, alert for any possible attack from the rear.

By the time they reached the foot of the hill, Frank and Joe had drawn close enough to their quarry to spot his shadowy figure disappearing into the ghost town. The boys trod stealthily on the snow-crusted wooden sidewalk, hugging the buildings. Ahead they could hear the man's footsteps and see his bulky, muffled shape. Suddenly he vanished into the sagging shell of a deserted building.

The Hardys quickened their pace and peered around the corner of the building. They were just in time to see the man emerge from the rear. He whirled about and ran to the far side of the adjoining building.

Frank darted in pursuit and saw the man return to the street. When Frank reached the sidewalk again, Joe was at his elbow, silent as a shadow. Ahead, the man was hurrying down the street towards the other end of town.

"He knows he's being followed," Joe whispered, "and is trying to shake us."

"Come on, or we'll lose him!" Frank urged.

Flinging caution aside, the boys broke into a run, their steps pounding on the plank walk. Apparently their quarry heard them and immediately stepped up his own pace. A moment later the dim figure melted into the darkness between two old buildings. Frank and Joe reached the spot in a few seconds.

"This way!" Frank urged in a low voice, and the Hardys plunged into the shadowy gloom of the narrow passageway.

Behind the two structures, the brothers found themselves in an area overgrown with weeds and brush which merged into the trees on the hillside. Frank and Joe halted, straining their eyes in the darkness and listening intently. Nothing could be heard but the wind—then the howl of a wolf somewhere beyond the ridge.

"Looks as if he's given us the slip," Joe muttered.

The boys flicked on their flashlights and searched about. They finally picked out the fugitive's prints, but his tracks led to the hard-trampled roadway and became indistinguishable. Baffled, the Hardys started back through the ghost town on their way to Hank's cabin.

"Of all the luck!" Joe grumbled. "We almost had our hands on that spy!"

"At least we've learned one thing about him," Frank said thoughtfully.

"What's that?"

"His nickname. The man he met in the cemetery called him 'Slip Gun'."

"You're right! I almost forgot," Joe said. "Maybe it'll help us trace him, if we can find out what it means. Any idea?"

Frank shook his head. "Not a glimmer, except that it sounds like a cowboy expression. Maybe Hank can tell us."

As they approached Ben Tinker's place, the brothers noticed that the windows were dark. Frank and Joe paused at the shack to listen, and heard a steady wheezing snore coming from inside.

"Good thing the old man's asleep"—Frank chuckled —"or he might have started shooting at us!"

The Hardys resumed their pace. They were about to go past the deserted dance hall next door, when suddenly they froze in their tracks. Both Frank and Joe felt the hair on their necks rise and cold chills sweep up and down their spines.

From the abandoned hall, through the moan of the wind, came the sound of piano playing.

Tinker's ghost music!

·7·

A Rooftop Struggle

THE wind suddenly died down and in the eerie silence Frank and Joe again heard the tinkle of the piano keys coming from the deserted dance hall.

Joe murmured, "Here's *one* mystery we can solve tonight! Let's find out what goes on in here!"

Moving lightly over the wooden sidewalk, the boys approached the dance-hall entrance. The weird, tuneless music stopped.

Frank and Joe looked at each other. "Maybe we've scared the spook away," Frank whispered half jokingly.

As if in answer, the music started once more. This time both the treble and bass keys of the piano sounded.

Quickly the Hardys drew flashlights from their jacket pockets and stepped inside. The searchers snapped on their flashlights and played the beams about the interior.

The music stopped again.

The room was sparsely furnished with a few rickety tables and chairs, heavily coated with dust. Ancient oil-lamp chandeliers, festooned with cobwebs, dangled from the ceiling.

At that moment the piano resumed its tinkling. Outside, the wind howled and shutters banged.

"Boy! This place is really creepy!" said Joe with a shudder.

Frank gripped his brother's arm. "Look there!"

The boys' lights now fell on a raised dais at one end of the room. On it stood a battered upright piano.

The Hardys stared in astonishment as the music continued. "The piano's playing by itself!" Joe exclaimed.

Quickly the brothers crossed the room and Frank lifted the top of the old piano. He shone his flashlight inside. There was a sudden squeaking and twanging of wires.

"For Pete's sake!" he burst out, as several rats scampered out of the piano, jumped down to the floor, and scurried away.

The boys laughed heartily. "There goes Tinker's ghost music," Frank said.

"Talented rats." Joe grinned.

Suddenly, from the direction of the doorway, they heard the sidewalk creak. The boys whirled as a low, flat voice snarled, "You kids have been askin' for it!"

Frank and Joe barely had time to glimpse a head—masked by a ghostlike hood with eyeholes—above the swinging doors. Then a gloved hand jerked into view, clutching a short-barrelled revolver, the thumb cocking back the hammer. There was a spurt of flame.

Bang! A bullet whistled across the room and thudded into the piano. The Hardys dived from the dais, snapping off their flashlights and crashing into the tables and chairs below.

As the echoes of the shot died away, Frank picked up a broken chair and hurled it in the general direction of the gun flash.

There was a grunt as the chair struck, then the

Hardys could hear the gunman's feet scraping across the floor. He was stalking them in the darkness!

The boys separated instinctively to divide his attention. Frank crept off to the right and Joe to the left.

Suddenly Frank sprang to his feet. In two long strides he reached the window and leaped through it into the darkness outside.

Crash! Bang! There was no glass in the window, but Frank's weight had carried away the crosspieces of the frame. He landed feet first. A moment later he saw a figure struggling through the window, grunting with the effort. The masked man!

Frank dashed around the corner of the dance hall. When he reached the back, he skidded to a halt at a high fence that was blocking his way. Hearing the gunman's steps behind him, Frank vaulted the fence and fell in a heap on the other side.

The gunman leaped a moment later. Frank held his breath. He could see the man silhouetted against the dim light of the sky—then darting off into the darkness.

Frank jumped up and dashed into a ramshackle building that stood next to the dance hall. But the hooded man evidently had spotted the boy's move, for Frank heard steps pounding in pursuit.

Without hesitation he raced through the front door and out on to the slippery, snowy sidewalk.

There was no time to find cover. The gunman was hot on his heels. In desperation, Frank ran straight down the open street. As he sped along, he wondered what had happened to Joe.

Flinging a glance over his shoulder, Frank saw the hooded gunman raise his arm to fire. *Zing!* The bullet whistled past Frank's head and ricocheted off a metal store sign.

Just ahead, to the left, was an old hitching rail. Frank recalled that it stood in front of the ghost town's abandoned hotel. He cut across the street and dashed into the narrow side yard of the hotel.

A flight of outside stairs slanted up the wall of the building. Frank mounted the steps two at a time. At the top was a rickety wooden balcony, which sagged under Frank's weight as he stepped on to it.

"Now what?" the young detective wondered. Had he worked himself into a corner? Frank's heart thudded as he heard the gunman's footsteps on the wooden walk below.

Just out of reach, the overhanging roof of the hotel loomed in the blackness. There was no place else to go, so Frank leaped up for the edge.

His fingers dug into the broken shingles and he swung himself on to the rear slope of the snow-covered roof. Meanwhile, the hooded gunman had already started up the stairs. Frank heard his clattering footsteps as he reached the balcony platform. Then he saw the man's hands appear, clutching the edge of the roof. A moment later his hooded head rose into view against the night sky! He was pulling himself up for a shot at close range!

Frank fought down a surge of panic. He had wriggled some distance away from the eaves. Now he must work his way back and try to overcome his assailant before the man could pull his gun.

Frank slithered towards him across the slippery

shingles. By now the man had one leg up over the roof
and was groping for the gun in his coat pocket.

"I won't be able to reach him in time!" Frank
thought grimly.

Just then he heard steps racing up the stairway to the
balcony.

The gunman heard the footsteps, too. He paused and
looked down, then managed to extract the gun from his
pocket. An instant later Frank saw his body jerk, and
the man clutched the roof edge as if to brace himself.

Evidently the newcomer was pulling the gunman's
other leg, trying to dislodge him! The hooded figure
suddenly gave a tremendous heave upward and the
next moment was free, sprawled full length on the roof.
Frank by now was close enough to grab the man's coat
sleeve.

The gunman threw up his arm and yanked it free.
But the force of this action caused him to lose his grip
completely! His gun flew through the air, hit the rear
part of the roof, and bounced off. The man, meanwhile
was rolling and slipping rapidly towards the edge.

Frank saw him clutch frantically for the gutter. The
man caught it, hung suspended for a moment, then
swung over to the drainpipe and slid down it to the
ground.

"Frank! Are you all right?" It *was* Joe!

"I'm okay." As quickly as possible, Frank wriggled
across the roof and dropped safely on to the balcony
platform.

The Hardys glanced over the railing. Below, the
hooded figure was groping about hastily, trying to find
his gun.

"Come on, Joe! Let's get him this time!" Frank urged, and the boys went rushing down the stairs.

Hearing them, the man gave up his search and dashed off into the darkness. Their quarry was some distance ahead when Frank and Joe approached the inhabited part of Lucky Lode. But the town was so dimly lit it was hard to keep the figure in view, except for his white hood.

The next moment the boys lost sight of him completely as he disappeared into the deep shadows around the general store. Nevertheless, Frank and Joe dashed in pursuit.

Reaching the store, they saw no one in front, so they ran to the back. The area was hidden in almost total darkness.

Suddenly Frank stiffened. "Did you hear something?" he muttered.

"Yes. Sounded like a door closing."

"Come on!"

The boys ran round to the front of the store. There were no lights showing. Joe grabbed the doorknob and shook it. The door was locked.

Frank knocked. The sound echoed loudly in the quiet of the deserted street. The boys waited for a few moments. When no one answered, Frank repeated his knock. He kept hammering on the door.

At last there was a response. From inside came the call, "Just a minute! Hold your horses!"

Presently a light showed, and a moment later Jim Burke came to the door, holding an oil lamp. He had pulled on a bathrobe over his underwear.

"Well? What's all the excitement about?" From the

look on his face, Burke was not pleased at being disturbed at so late an hour. Frank explained why they had roused him.

"Nope." Burke's expression was puzzled as he shook his head. "I haven't seen or heard anyone—except you two."

"Could the fellow we're after have slipped in your back door?" Joe asked.

"Not a chance," Burke replied. "I sleep right in the back room."

As Burke spoke, the front door suddenly burst open and Bob Dodge strode in out of the windy darkness.

Frank and Joe stared at him. Dodge's outer garments were wet with snow, and his coat sleeves and trouser legs were covered with burrs!

· 8 ·

Tommy-knockers!

THE same thought struck the Hardy boys. Did the burrs on Dodge's clothes mean he had been one of the people in the cemetery—perhaps even the man they had chased? Excited, Frank and Joe watched the big man's face closely.

But Dodge displayed no outward signs of guilt. "What's all the shooting about?" he asked while brushing the snow off his coat.

Burke raised his eyebrows. "You heard it?"

"I sure did," the big, white-haired man replied. "I couldn't sleep tonight, so I went for a stroll up on the hillside. Then I heard two gunshots and I came down to investigate."

"Did you see anybody, Mr Dodge?" Frank put in.

"Well, not too clearly. I thought I glimpsed two people running in this direction. But when I got down to the street, there was no one in sight."

"Must've been these two lads," the storekeeper said. "They woke me up and told me some gunslinger had been chasin' 'em through the ghost town. Didn't hear anythin' myself," Burke added, "but I guess I was pretty sound asleep."

Frank repeated the story they had told Burke. "We

were investigating what Ben Tinker had told us about the old dance hall being haunted," Frank explained. "While we were inside the place, someone shot at us."

"He chased us for a while, and then we turned the tables and started chasing him," Joe added. "Whoever the man was, he headed for the store."

Dodge frowned worriedly. "You boys seem to attract danger. I hope you won't take any unnecessary chances on this case."

"We'll try not to," Frank said. "There isn't much more we can do tonight, anyhow."

The Hardys started to leave. Just before they reached the door, Frank turned and said casually, "By the way, does either of you know what's meant by a 'slip gun'?"

Dodge and Burke looked surprised, but otherwise their expressions seemed innocent enough.

"It's a gun that's been fixed in a certain way so it can be fired by thumbing the hammer," Dodge explained.

"You mean like fanning?" Joe asked.

"No. Fanning is when you hold the gun in one hand and keep knocking back the hammer with the other," Dodge replied. "But in slip shooting you fire the gun by simply wiping your thumb back over the hammer. It's a bit slower than fanning, but more accurate."

"How would a gun be fixed for slip shooting?" Frank put in.

Dodge shrugged. "Oh, often the trigger's taken out, and the hammer spur lowered. Sometimes a slip shooter may cut off part of the barrel so he can carry the gun in his pocket."

"Sounds like a real gunfighter's trick," Joe said.

"You boys aimin' to try it?" Burke grinned.

"No," Joe replied. "I just meant that a slip gun isn't something a law-abiding person would be apt to have around."

"Ever seen one?" Frank asked the two men.

Burke promptly shook his head. Dodge looked a bit startled, then answered slowly, "No. Stop to think of it, I don't even recall where I acquired that information. One of those things you pick up in the West, I suppose."

The boys said goodbye and went out. The night was chillier than ever and the wind biting.

"Where to?" Joe asked, pulling his jacket collar up for protection. "Back to Hank's?"

"Not yet," Frank said. "Let's see if we can find that gun the hooded man dropped."

"Hey, that's right!"

As the two headed back towards the ghost town, Frank said thoughtfully, "Looks as though we now have two prime suspects, Joe."

"Right—Burke, or Bob Dodge, which is hard to believe. But those burrs on his clothes sure looked suspicious."

"Dodge admitted he was on the hillside," Frank pointed out. "I suppose the cemetery isn't the only place they grow."

"You'll have to admit, though, it's a real coincidence," Joe argued. "On the other hand, Burke took a long time to open the door for us."

Frank nodded. "Long enough to yank off a hood and get out of wet clothes. I wish we could have searched his back room."

"Another thing," Joe went on, "the general store would be a perfect set up for a spy of Big Al's in Lucky Lode."

"It sure would," Frank agreed. "Burke has a chance to learn everything that goes on. What's more, he could relay telephone or telegraph messages between Big Al and members of the gang in other spots—even handle mail for them."

"He could provide Big Al with supplies, too, including that red paint."

The boys trudged along in silence.

"We *can* build just as strong a case against Dodge," Frank said after a while. "It seems strange to me that he keeps hanging around Lucky Lode, instead of tending to his business in Helena."

"I've wondered about that, too," Joe conceded, "even though he claims to be staying here on account of the case Dad's working on. If Dodge is in cahoots with the gang, he may be keeping an eye on the gang's doings. Also, he could be using the 'copter to transport supplies to the crooks."

"And don't forget that shotgun booby trap at the airport," Frank added. "Dodge sent us to the 'copter alone—which could mean he wanted to make sure he wasn't in range when the gun went off."

Joe frowned. "But would a company president plot with a crook to rob his own truck?"

"Why not? The money was covered by insurance. And he might have hired Dad to allay suspicion."

As the boys neared the old abandoned hotel, they watched the display of northern lights sweeping across the sky.

"You know, Frank," Joe said slowly, "there's one big thing in Dodge's favour."

"What's that?"

"Dad likes him."

"You're right," Frank agreed. "From the way Dad spoke last night, he really admires Dodge—and Dad's a good judge of character. He never would have talked about Dodge as he did if he suspected him."

Making their way through the side yard to the back of the hotel, the Hardys switched on their flashlights and began searching for the gun.

Presently Joe exclaimed, "Here it is!" The revolver lay in a clump of undergrowth. Joe picked it up carefully by the trigger guard.

"It's a slip gun, all right," Frank commented. "No trigger, and the barrel's been cut short."

"That means Slip Gun is the man we followed from the cemetery! He's Big Al's spy."

"Yes," Frank agreed. "You know, Joe—Dodge *might* have been the person we heard following *us*."

"Maybe, but there's no way to be sure," Joe pointed out. "Slip Gun is a husky fellow, and Dodge and Burke are both big men. Either one would answer the description."

"True enough," Frank conceded. "Besides, if Dodge did follow us, why didn't he admit it?"

When the Hardys got back to the cabin, both their father and Hank were sleeping soundly. Frank and Joe checked the slip gun for fingerprints, but found none clear enough to photograph. Evidently the hooded man's gloved hand had smudged any that might have existed before the night's events.

The brothers undressed quickly and crawled into their bunks. As Joe blew out the oil lamp, Frank yawned and said sleepily, "Wonder what 'Shadow of the Bear' means?"

"Me too. Something else to track down—" Joe's voice trailed off and he was fast asleep.

Neither boy needed an alarm clock. They got up at dawn without disturbing the men and had a quick breakfast. Then they went outside, saddled up their horses, and mounted.

"Do you have Hank's sketch of the mines?" Joe asked as they started up the hill.

"Right here." Frank patted his pocket. "I wish we still had Mike Onslow's map."

"Poor Mike!" Joe reined in his skittish horse. "I wish we could find at least some of his missing gold."

"So do I." Frank added with a chuckle, "I'll bet Aunt Gertrude is fussing over him right now like a mother hen."

When the boys reached the top of the hill, they could see the sunlight starting to work its way over Windy Peak. "Lucky Slip Gun didn't stop us," said Joe as they halted to study the map.

Brady's Mine, they found, was located to the north, not far away. Half an hour's ride brought them to a point somewhere below the mine site. Here the boys dismounted and led their horses carefully up the slope.

Frank and Joe scouted the area, but could see nobody, nor any tracks in the snow.

"Let's take a look inside," Joe suggested.

The boys tied their horses to a clump of bushes a hundred yards from the mouth of the mine. After making sure their flashlights were working, they cautiously approached the dark hole in the edge of the hill.

The mine entrance was big enough for them to walk erect. Inside, the Hardys paused to listen, then snapped on their flashlights. They were in a fair-sized cavern, which had been hacked and blasted out of the mountainside. Just ahead, a tunnel sloped downward into darkness.

Among the rubble on the floor were some lengths of rusty iron pipe and a discarded pick with a broken handle.

"Doesn't look as if anyone has been here in a long time," Joe murmured. His voice echoed weirdly in the chilly cavern.

Frank was about to reply when suddenly both boys stiffened. "Did you hear something?" he whispered.

"I sure did!"

As the brothers froze into silence, the sound came again—*tap . . . tap-tap . . . tap.*

"Spirits!" Joe gasped. "Tommy-knockers!"

·9·

The Crowbar Clue

THE tapping noises from within the mine died away. Frank and Joe looked at each other uncertainly.

"You don't really believe that superstition about spirit rapping?" Frank muttered.

"Of course not," Joe whispered. "It did sound spooky, though."

"More likely it's Big Al's gang," Frank said, peering around intently.

Joe's face took on a troubled frown. "But there were no prints outside showing that anyone else had come here."

"Maybe there's another entrance," Frank argued. "Let's find out."

The two boys started forward into the tunnel. Its walls and ceiling were shored with ancient timbers that gave out a smell of mouldy dampness. The passageway not only sloped downward, but turned and twisted. Evidently it had been tunnelled out to follow the vein of ore.

Presently the floor of the passage levelled off. The Hardys probed the darkness ahead with the yellow glow of their flashlights. Still there was no sign of the tunnel coming to an end or opening out into a large excavation.

"How far does this go?" Joe said tensely.

"It has to end somewhere," Frank replied.

Both boys felt their nerves tauten. The eerie stillness was broken only by the sound of their footsteps echoing hollowly through the tunnel.

Suddenly Frank came to a halt and pointed to the handle of a crowbar protruding from between two of the wall timbers. The bar was painted with bright-red markings. The Hardys bent close to examine them.

$$AL-5-X-*-4$$

" 'Al!' " Joe read. "This may be a code message from Big Al to the gang!"

"Or maybe a message *to* Big Al," Frank countered. He tested one of the red daubs with his finger. The paint was dry but looked fresh enough to have been applied recently.

Joe tried to puzzle out the meaning of the message. "Any ideas, Frank?"

The older boy shook his head. "Beats me—unless," he added slowly, "the crowbar was put here to mark a certain spot in the mine."

"Maybe something's hidden behind the timbers!" Joe conjectured excitedly.

Frank doubted this. "These shorings look as if they've been here forever."

"Let's make sure," Joe urged. "We'll want to take the crowbar along with us, anyhow, so we can check it for clues. Hold my flashlight, will you?"

Gripping the handle carefully, so that at least part of the surface could be tested later for fingerprints, Joe yanked hard on the crowbar. It gave scarcely at all. He threw his whole weight into the effort and began forcing the bar from side to side. The timbering creaked ominously.

"Hey, be careful!" Frank warned. "This tunnel isn't shored up too solidly along here!"

"Don't worry—I can get the bar out." Joe grunted, heaving hard. "It's coming now!"

The rotten wood crumpled and shredded as the crowbar gouged into it. Suddenly, as Joe gave one last hard yank, there was a loud splintering noise. The ceiling sagged.

"Look out!" Frank cried out. He grabbed Joe's arm, and both boys leaped ahead in the nick of time.

A split second later the tunnel caved in! As the boys dashed to safety, tons of earth and rock came pouring down. The passageway rumbled and thundered with the deafening impact.

"Good grief!" Joe stared back in awe after he and his brother had come to a halt deeper inside the tunnel. "I should have listened to your warning, Frank!"

"Forget it. Let's be thankful neither of us got hurt and that I still have our flashlights."

Both boys coughed and tried to screen their noses from the cloud of dust billowing through the passage. Gradually the particles settled.

"How do we get out of here?" Joe asked worriedly. "Dig our way through?"

The brothers strode back towards the scene of the cave-in. The tunnel there was totally blocked by the tremendous fall of dirt and rock.

"What about the crowbar?" Frank asked suddenly. "We can use that."

"I dropped it," Joe admitted, red-faced. "It's some-where underneath all this rubble."

"Oh, great."

"Maybe we can still dig through," Joe said. "Come on—let's try!"

The Hardys set their flashlights on the ground, then began clawing away the debris with their hands. Soon the boys were panting and soaked with perspiration. In addition to loose dirt and stones, huge hunks of rock had broken off and been carried downward in the cave-in.

After trying vainly to shift one enormous stone fragment, Frank and Joe gave up in despair.

"We'll never make it," Frank said, breathing hard. "We don't even know how far the cave-in extends."

Joe leaned against the wall to collect his strength. "That means we'll *have* to find another way out of here."

"If there is one."

Although neither boy said so aloud, they knew their situation was desperate. Brady's Mine was only one of the places on Hank's map which they had picked out to search and they had told no one of the clue they had overheard. No doubt a search party would be organized when they failed to return. But how long would they be trapped underground before help might arrive?

"No use standing here," Frank said finally. "Let's find out where the tunnel leads."

"Right. We're getting fresh air, so there must be an exit."

Using only one flashlight in order to conserve their battery power, the Hardys pressed on.

"Joe, there's another reason why we'll find an exit," Frank said suddenly. "I believe someone from the gang was doing that tapping. If so, he must have been on this side of the cave-in."

"Sure—and the noises we heard were the sounds of the crowbar being pounded into position," Joe guessed.

"Let's hope he hasn't heard us," Frank murmured. "And the chances are there was more than one member of the gang here."

"Probably they scooted out the other entrance, so they wouldn't be caught in the cave-in," Joe reasoned. "But we'd better talk in whispers just the same."

Both boys realized also that the flashlight beam would make them easy targets. But they had no choice. Without a light to guide them, there would be no hope of finding a way out through the inky darkness.

Presently the tunnel widened, opening into a sizable cavern. The Hardys held their breath as Frank swept his flashlight beam rapidly about the chamber. He and Joe were ready to dive to the floor or retreat at the first sign of an enemy. But the cavern was empty.

"Look!" Frank exclaimed. "Another tunnel!" He aimed his light towards a dark hole that gaped in the far wall.

The two boys hurried to examine it. This passageway was narrower than the one they had just left and not shored by timbers. It was high enough for the Hardys to walk erect, but in places they found it a tight squeeze.

This time, Joe took the lead. Although the tunnel twisted and turned, he pressed forward steadily. He became aware that the cool draught was growing stronger.

"Feel the breeze?" Joe called back over his shoulder. "We must be near the end."

Joe had spoken too soon. They turned a sharp corner and the tunnel ended in a sheer wall of solid rock.

They could go no farther!

The boys shone their flashlights upward. There was nothing to see but the rock roof.

Joe gave a groan and sank down on the rocky floor of the tunnel. "What'll we do now?"

For a few minutes the brothers sat in silence. Then suddenly Frank leaped to his feet. "The draught!" he said.

"What about it?"

"We've passed the opening."

Frank snapped on his light and started back down the tunnel. Joe scrambled to his feet and followed. As they moved back around the bend again, they could feel the movement of air on their cheeks.

"The air current seems to flow from somewhere up above," Frank said, aiming his light towards the roof.

"It does!" Joe exclaimed. "See that crack?"

High overhead, well out of reach, was a rocky shelf protruding from the wall. Frank grabbed a handful of dust and tossed it up to the shelf. Some dropped on the edge, but the rest remained in the air and then slowly drifted away out of sight.

"That's it!" Joe said excitedly. "There's something beyond! It must lead to an exit."

Frank braced himself against the wall. "Up you go, Joe!"

Quickly Joe climbed to his brother's shoulders and found he could easily reach the rocky shelf. Joe gripped the edge and pulled himself upward. Then he lay on his stomach and, reaching down, grasped Frank's hand in a fireman's grip. A second later Frank was seated beside Joe.

When the Hardys turned, they found still another tunnel facing them. This one slanted upward from the shelf and was too low-roofed for anyone to walk upright. Aiming their lights ahead, the boys crawled on hands and knees through the cramped area.

Presently a glimmer of daylight showed ahead. Joe was about to exclaim in relief when a murmur of voices suddenly reached the boys' ears.

The Hardys knelt motionless and looked at each other. Were members of the gang just outside the tunnel exit waiting for them?

Frank put a finger to his lips. Without a word the boys resumed their crawling—but more slowly and quietly now—towards the mouth of the passage.

Near the opening they halted. A voice which Frank and Joe recognized as that of the thin man they had overheard at the cemetery was saying:

"Those kids ought to be showin' any time now, if the cave-in didn't get 'em."

Then another man, deeper-voiced, chuckled. "If it didn't, we'll trap 'em like rats comin' out of a hole!"

·10·

Ambush Trail

A PANG of fear shot through Frank and Joe as they realized they were trapped in the mine. A clump of brush partly screened the tunnel mouth, but the Hardys' enemies were waiting outside—ready to seize the boys the moment they appeared!

Scarcely daring to breathe, the boys listened as the thin man went on: "I figured it was them Hardys eavesdroppin' at the graveyard last night." He laughed. "Pretty smart o' me givin' out that hint about Brady's Mine, eh?"

"They fell for it, all right," his partner agreed. "And that crowbar business, too, with the phony code. Best part is, it'll look accidental."

The boys heard a deep-throated chuckle. Joe shot a shamefaced glance at his brother. The crowbar must have been painted to attract their attention and then cunningly planted at a weakly shored part of the tunnel!

The thin man continued, "I'll really get a kick out o' payin' off those brats. Big Al was plenty sore at me 'cause that shotgun set up in the 'copter didn't work out."

" 'Twasn't your fault, Slim."

"Try tellin' that to Al. He was mad over Slip Gun

not gettin' the kids last night. Now he blames me for wastin' time this mornin'."

"How come?"

"Aw, that special business he keeps harpin' on—it's all he thinks about. He wanted us to do some searchin' elsewhere today, but the Hardys comin' here changed his plans."

There was silence for a while. Frank and Joe waited tensely, digesting what they had overheard. Then Slim spoke again.

"Wonder how much longer we'll have to wait? I'm gettin' fed up, perchin' here in this cold."

"Maybe the kids can't find their way out," his partner suggested. "If they ain't dead already, that is."

"You sure the tunnel caved in, Jake?"

"Sure. Sounded like an earthquake. I could see the dust comin' out the front end."

"Did you make certain the tunnel was completely blocked?" Slim asked.

"Well, I didn't actually go inside and look. I might've got trapped. Besides, they didn't show up!"

"You chowderhead!" Slim exploded irritably. "If it ain't blocked, the kids may still be able to squirm out. Go on back and make sure."

"Okay, okay." Jake sounded as if he were getting to his feet.

"Wait! Got another idea. You fetch their horses and bring 'em back here before you check the tunnel," Slim added. "That way, there'll be no chance o' the Hardys pullin' a sneak."

After warning Joe to silence, Frank wriggled forward

and peered out through the screen of brush. In the
distance he could see Jake's stocky figure heading down
the snow-covered mountainside on his way to the mine
entrance.

Frank was astonished at how far Jake had gone in a
few seconds. Since the two men had conversed in low
voices, the speakers had sounded as if they were fairly
close to the clump of brush. Now Frank realized his
mistake.

The opening was on one side of a narrow draw. Slim
was evidently perched out of sight, somewhere higher
up the mountainside—probably holding a rifle to cover
the boys.

The two men must have thought their conversation
was inaudible to anyone else, but the steep-sided draw
had caused an echo effect, trapping their voices and
reflecting the sound back towards the tunnel.

Frank signalled his brother to crawl forward and
join him. Stealthily Joe complied. Several minutes later
Jake returned, leading the boys' horses. Slim came
down the slope to meet him.

"No sign of 'em," the Hardys heard Jake report.

"Check inside the tunnel," Slim told his partner.
"If they didn't get buried by the cave-in, we're
supposed to take 'em up to Windy Peak."

The thugs exchanged one or two other remarks, but
their conversation was carried away by a surge of icy
wind sweeping down the draw.

Jake turned and started off again, heading back to
the mine entrance. Slim threw a glance towards the
clump of brush to make sure their quarry had not yet
emerged. Then he took the boys' horses and trudged

towards a stunted, leafless tree growing out of the mountainside.

"Let's jump him!" Joe urged.

Frank had noticed that the man wore a long-barrelled revolver in a holster slung at his hip. If he had a rifle, he must have left it at the spot where he and Jake had been waiting.

"It's risky, but we'll try," Frank agreed.

The moaning of the wind would help cover the sound of their footsteps in the snow, and Slim's back was turned as he prepared to tether the horses to the tree. Jake was already out of sight behind a shoulder of the hill.

"It's now or never!" Frank hissed.

Slithering from the hole and past the screen of brush, the boys darted across the slope. They were halfway to the man when one of the horses suddenly detected the boys and whinnied.

Slim muttered an oath and jerked the horse roughly by its bridle. He seemed to realize that something behind him had startled the animal.

The man whirled, his hand streaking towards the gun at his hip. At the same moment, Frank hurled himself through the air in a flying tackle. Just as Slim yanked his gun from its holster, Frank rammed into him!

In an instant Joe had joined the fray. He stunned Slim with a backhand smash to the side of the head. As the thug went limp, his revolver arched into the air and went hurtling down the mountainside.

"Come on! Grab your horse!" Joe urged. "We've got to get out of here before Jake finds out what has happened and starts firing at us."

The boys quickly untied their mounts and swung into the saddles. The horses whinnied, then went galloping down the draw as Frank and Joe dug their heels into the horses' flanks.

Frank threw a glance over his shoulder just in time to see Slim staggering to his feet. The man's face was livid with fury.

"Jake!" he bawled at the top of his lungs. "The Hardy kids are gettin' away!"

His voice trailed off and was lost against the wind. Moments later a rifle crack echoed, but by now the boys were well out of range.

"Did you spot the men's horses?" Joe called.

"Up the mountainside, I think," Frank yelled back. "We'd better not count on a big lead!"

The boys pushed their mounts hard, taking desperate chances along the rocky declivities. No sounds of pursuit reached their ears, and gradually Frank and Joe slowed their pace.

In twenty minutes they topped the ridge overlooking Lucky Lode and rode down the trail into town. As their horses clip-clopped along the main street towards Hank's cabin, Frank asked, "Did you hear what that fellow Slim said about taking us to Windy Peak?"

"I sure did," Joe returned. "It could mean that's Al's hideout. Let's search there."

Frank nodded. "It'll be an overnight trip. We'll need supplies."

The boys were surprised to find a battered blue station wagon parked in front of their cabin.

"Doc Whitlow's here," Hank explained when they went inside. "He's in with your pa now."

"Is Dad worse?" Frank asked, concerned.

"Not exactly, but he spent a kind o' restless night. And this mornin' he felt like he was runnin' a slight fever. So I fetched the doc."

Minutes later the physician, a young man with a brown beard, emerged from Mr Hardy's room.

"Nothing to worry about," Doc Whitlow announced. "Apparently your father overexerted himself yesterday and irritated the fracture."

"He shouldn't have worked on the wall," Frank said.

"I gave him something to ease the pain," the doctor said. "He's sleeping now."

Doc Whitlow declined Hank's offer of lunch, saying he had to get back to his office in the nearby town of Bear Creek. After he had left, Hank prepared a meal of beans and frankfurters and sat down to eat with Frank and Joe.

"You boys just missed seein' Bob Dodge," he remarked.

"When was he here?" Joe asked.

"Just a while 'fore you two showed up. Say—you boys look like you been through the mill. What happened?"

The Hardys related all that had taken place the night before, as well as the entrapment at Brady's Mine and their narrow escape from the two gang members, Slim and Jake. Hank, too, was puzzled by the Shadow of the Bear reference. The boys asked him to pass on a full report to their father.

"You mean you won't be around to tell him?"

"We're going up to investigate Windy Peak," Frank replied. "The sooner the better."

A worried look spread over the Westerner's leathery face. He urged the boys to be extremely cautious, now that the gang was clearly trying to get rid of them. He agreed to provide supplies for the trip, however, and to lend them his mare Daisy for use as a pack horse. Soon the boys were ready to start.

"What's the easiest way to get up Windy Peak, Hank?" asked Joe as he tightened the cinch.

"There ain't no easy way this time o' year," the man replied. "You'll have to take an old Indian path called Ambush Trail, up near Brady's Mine. Starts about half a mile north o' the entrance. But watch your step."

"Bad going?" Frank put in.

"Plenty bad. Even in summer, that trail's full o' narrow ledges and hairpin turns. Now it'll be lots worse. We had a freak thaw early this month that probably loosened quite a few boulders. Some places you'll be on icy ledges lookin' straight down the side of a cliff."

Hank's warning proved to be fully justified. At first the trail seemed fairly easy, but as they left the timber-line behind, the path narrowed and wound confusingly in and out among the rocky outcrops on the face of the mountainside.

"I'll bet even the Indians got lost sometimes on this snaky trail," Joe remarked wryly.

On their left the mountain towered sheer above them, with precariously poised boulders and crusted drifts of snow. Half-dislodged clumps of earth and rock projected from the cliffside.

"This would be a bad place to get caught in an avalanche," Frank observed.

Joe gulped. "Whew! Don't even *think* it!"

Presently the boys saw horseshoe prints in the snow. Apparently the riders, whoever they were, had cut in from some side path.

"At least we seem to be on the right trail," Joe said tensely.

"Probably members of the gang," Frank cautioned. "We'd better keep a sharp look out."

The prints faded out presently as the path became more glazed and rocky. Soon the trail narrowed so much that the boys were forced to proceed single file. Both gulped as they glanced down the cliff at the icy river below.

Joe was close behind when Frank turned a sharp corner on the trail and reined to a halt. Ahead was a huge barrier of snow, rocks, and logs.

"Must have been an avalanche," Joe said.

Frank moved forward for a better look. "Maybe not," he commented. "Those logs don't look like windfalls—they could have been cut by men. Anyhow —our trail is blocked."

After sizing up the situation, Frank and Joe decided to risk skirting the curve of the hillside, which seemed less steep at this point.

"Maybe we can get back on the trail somewhere beyond the barrier," Joe said hopefully.

Dismounting, the Hardys started cautiously downward. Frank went first, leading his horse and Daisy. Joe followed with his mount.

For a while the footing seemed fairly sure. The Hardys had negotiated their way around part of the slope when Frank suddenly felt the ground shifting beneath his feet.

"Look out, Joe!" he cried out. "There's loose shale under this snow!"

A spatter of stones and earth went clattering down the mountainside. As the brothers scrambled for safer ground, their mounts became panicky, neighing and pawing wildly for a foothold.

The horses' bucking dislodged still more shale. The next instant, the horses and the boys went slipping and sliding downward in the landslide. All three of the animals went over on their sides in a swirl of flying hoofs.

Frank and Joe were half stunned as they tumbled on down the mountain. Below was an icy creek. Suddenly they were sailing through the air.

Crash! . . . Crash!

The Hardys and their horses shattered the ice and disappeared below the surface of the mountain torrent!

·11·

Shadow of the Bear

THE icy shock of the water stung the Hardys back to full consciousness. They flailed their arms and legs wildly, fighting to get to the surface.

Frank broke water first, gasping for breath. His heart skipped when he saw nothing but the half-frozen river, the struggling horses, and the steep-sided canyon. Where was Joe?

Then his brother bobbed to the surface nearby. "Thank goodness," Frank murmured.

Neither boy had breath to spare to make himself heard above the roar of the rushing current. The ice extended outward from both banks, but near the centre, the water was surging along in full torrent. With every passing moment, Frank and Joe were being swept farther downstream.

Joe pointed to the horses. The two saddle animals were breaking their way through the ice, gradually swimming and floundering towards shore. Daisy, the elderly pack mare, loaded down with supplies, was having a more difficult time.

"She may drown!" Frank thought fearfully.

He and Joe summoned all their strength and swam towards the frantic animals. In a few minutes their own horses managed to reach the bank. Daisy was rolling her eyes, whinnying and snorting with terror. But Frank and Joe were finally able to steer her to safety through the broken ice.

At last the boys staggered out of the water and flopped down on the rocky, snow-covered bank. The saddle horses stood shaking themselves farther up the shore, and Daisy trotted on to join them.

"Wow!" Joe took a deep breath. "What a day for a swim!"

"Joe, we're pretty lucky, at that." Frank got up. "We'd better see about the supplies."

"And a fire—if we can make one," Joe added.

Both boys were shivering and blue with cold. They hurried towards the horses. At least half the provisions and gear strapped to Daisy's back had come loose and had been carried away.

"Let's get out of sight first," Joe suggested. "Someone may be spying on us from up on the mountain."

"Right!" Frank agreed. "I'm sure now that the barrier on the trail was no accident."

The brothers led the horses towards some sheltering timber. Just beyond the trees they discovered a rocky recess in the mountainside. Here they grouped the horses and proceeded to survey the state of their supplies.

"Well," Joe said, "at least it's not so bad as it might have been."

Most of their provisions were gone, as well as their tent and other camp equipment. But they had blankets, towels, spare clothing, fishing gear, compass, matches, and some food. Luckily, everything had been packed in waterproof wrapping.

"I'm sure glad we still have that compass," Frank remarked, as the boys unsaddled the horses and used the towels to rub down the animals.

"You bet," Joe agreed. "If we should lose our bearings in this wilderness with our food so low, we'd really be in a jam."

"You build a fire, Joe," Frank suggested, "while I get out dry clothes for us."

After donning fresh clothing in the warmth of the crackling flames, and drying their jackets, the Hardys soon felt more comfortable. Their horses recovered rapidly and began to nibble the shrubs and winter-dry brush sticking up through the snow.

Frank stepped out of their rocky niche and shaded his eyes towards the sun, which was already red and low in the sky. In another half hour it would be out of sight behind the mountains.

"Too late to do much travelling now," said Frank. "We may as well camp here and strike out for Windy Peak early in the morning."

"Okay, Frank. I'll try some fishing. That looks like a trout stream."

He put their collapsible fishing rod together and headed off among the trees towards the bank of the river.

"Watch your step on that ice!" Frank called.

As Joe disappeared from view, his brother took out their precious compass. Using the setting sun as a reference, he checked the action of the needle to see if any magnetic ore in the range might be affecting it. The deviation, if any, seemed to be very slight.

"It's a cinch we'll never get back up the cliff to the

trail," Frank thought. "At least not here. We'll have to follow the river and try to find some place where the canyon walls are not so steep."

"Frank! Frank!" It was Joe calling from the river. "Help! Frank, help!"

"The ice!" Frank thought. "Joe's broken through!"

Laying the compass on a flat rock, the older Hardy dashed towards the river. To Frank's amazement, Joe was in no danger. But he was sprawled flat on the ice, clinging desperately to the rod and trying not to lose the prize catch he had hooked. The fish had sounded and was bending the rod almost to a U-shape as it fought to escape.

"Quick! Give me a hand!" Joe shouted.

Frank flat-footed gingerly out on to the ice, grabbed the line, and began hauling in.

"I guess we're breaking all the rules for game fishing," he called back with a chuckle, "but this is one fellow we can't risk losing!"

The fish put up a furious struggle that roused the boys' admiration, but they finally managed to reel in a huge trout.

"Boy, what a swell catch!" Frank cried. "There's our supper!"

"First fish that ever decked me," Joe said, grinning. "But then it's the first time I've ever tried trout fishing on ice."

Back at camp, Joe set about cleaning the fish while Frank built up the fire. Suddenly Joe heard his brother gasp.

"What's wrong?"

"The compass!" Frank exclaimed. "I left it right

here on this flat rock. And now it's gone!"

"Are you sure?"

"Positive. I put it exactly where this pine cone is. Wait a minute! That wasn't here before!" Frank broke off and picked up the pine cone. An exasperated look spread over his face. "You know what, Joe? A pack rat has been here!"

"I'll bet you're right!" Joe declared. "The rat picked up the compass because it's bright and shiny, and left the pine cone in its place."

The Hardys looked at each other gravely. Any other time the situation might have been funny, but right now the compass was vital to them. Without it, they might never find their way safely out of the wilderness.

"Come on! Let's look for it!" Frank urged. "I remember reading that pack rats will often drop a prize if something else catches their eye."

The boys began a systematic search, pacing back and forth around the camp in widening circles. At last Frank detected some faint rodent tracks in the trampled snow and soon spotted a shiny object in the cliffside brush.

Frank pounced on the compass with a cry of relief. "Whew!" he exclaimed. "What a break!"

"Better keep it in your pocket from now on," Joe advised.

The trout, cooked over heated rocks, made a tasty dish. After the meal, the boys felt more cheerful. As they huddled around the campfire in their blankets, Frank said thoughtfully, "Tomorrow's the day for Big Al's meeting."

"Right. I wish we could find the place."

"If only we knew what Shadow of the Bear meant," Frank mused.

In spite of the cold and their desperate situation, the boys slept well. The horses, too, evidently rested well during the night, staying close together near the embers of the fire.

Next morning Frank and Joe made a cold breakfast of oatmeal mush and dried apricots from their scanty supplies. Then they fed and saddled the horses, strapped their remaining gear on Daisy's back, and headed downriver.

The canyon turned and twisted along the curve of the mountainside, and the footing was treacherous. As they rode, the Hardys continually scanned the sides of the gorge, hoping to find a route out of the canyon. Twice they dismounted and tried to thread their way upward, leading the horses. But both times the cliff wall proved too steep.

At last, however, the canyon opened out and the slope of the cliffs became more gentle. Relieved, Frank and Joe halted for another cold meal. Then they rode to higher ground and struck back across the rolling foothills of the mountain range in the general direction of town.

Eventually they cut into a beaten trail. About mid-afternoon, the brothers swung over a rise on the rocky, snow-covered path and Frank reined up sharply.

"Look!" he exclaimed, and indicated the area to their right.

Looming against the sky was a huge, ungainly rock formation that crudely resembled a bear standing upright.

"Al's meeting place!" Joe breathed.

Dismounting, the boys ground-hitched their horses out of sight behind a clump of boulders. Then they crept cautiously towards the huge rock formation. To their surprise, Frank and Joe discovered that it was poised on the rim of a small box canyon.

The Hardys cautiously peered over the edge. The canyon was choked with drifted snow, from which protruded a few scrubby trees and brush. The view directly below was blocked by a shelving overhang of rock, about twenty feet farther down and extending along the cliff wall. The boys could detect no sign or sound of human beings.

"Maybe we missed the meeting," Joe murmured. "Or this isn't the place, after all."

"I'll bet it is," Frank replied. "My guess is, the confab hasn't been held yet." He gazed across the canyon. "Let's keep an eye on that bear's shadow."

In the setting sun the rock formation cast a formless shadow on the opposite wall. As the boys stood up, Joe remarked with a puzzled look, "That shadow doesn't look much like a bear."

"True. But it might at some other time of day. Remember, Slim didn't name any hour for the meeting. He just said, 'Shadow of the Bear'."

"I get it!" Joe broke in excitedly. "Maybe the meeting is to take place when the bear shows up clearly on the canyon wall!"

"And that ought to be when the sun drops a little lower," Frank added.

Joe asked, "Do you think the meeting will be down inside the canyon?"

"Probably. Up here by this rock formation the gang would be too easy to spot."

"But this looks like a blind canyon to me," Joe objected. "How'll they get into it?"

"There may be an entrance we can't see from here. Let's stay out of sight."

The boys found cover in a nearby cluster of rocks and brush. As the sun sank lower, the bear's shadow across the canyon became more distinct and realistic.

"Listen!" Joe whispered suddenly.

From somewhere below came a clopping of horses' hoofs—then a sound of men reining up and dismounting. The Hardys peered downwards, but the rocky overhang of the canyon prevented them from seeing what was taking place.

A murmur of voices came drifting up. The boys strained their ears and recognized Slim's voice, but could not make out what he was saying. Then a harsh voice, unfamiliar to the Hardys, spoke out clearly:

"You sure muffed things in Lucky Lode, Slip Gun!"

"I couldn't help it, Big Al," returned a voice too muffled to identify.

"One more job like that and I'll—" the harsh tone faded to a threatening mutter.

Frank and Joe could hardly keep from shouting for joy. They had found Big Al! If only they could dare to try capturing him!

Big Al's Orders

THE only reply to Big Al's scornful words was a brief, sullen mutter. It was so low that the Hardys could not distinguish whether the speaker might have been Burke or Bob Dodge.

Frank and Joe exchanged a grimace of disappointment. If only the Lucky Lode spy would speak again, and more loudly! But evidently he was too cowed by his boss's angry tone to put up an argument.

"Stupid cluck!" Big Al continued to rant. "You had a chance to get rid of those kids—or at least scare 'em off this case. And what happens? You get so rattled you can't even hang on to your own gun!"

"Don't worry, Al"—Jake's voice cut in quickly, trying to placate the gang leader—"Slim and me took care o' them brats."

"At Brady's Mine?" the boss snapped back.

"Well, no—not there. The crowbar stunt worked okay, but they ducked the cave-in and—"

Jake's explanation was cut short by another outburst from Big Al. Slim hastened to soothe him.

"Jake's tryin' to tell you, boss—they're both drowned."

"Drowned?"

"Yeah. We figured they'd be comin' along Ambush Trail, so we fixed up a roadblock to sidetrack 'em and make 'em go lower down. The cliff shoulder along there is all loose shale, but it's covered over with snow. Sure enough, they tried to worm around it and the ground gave way. Must've been a regular landslide from the looks of it!" Slim chuckled with satisfaction. "Anyhow, they took a long fall and wound up in the drink, horses and all."

"You sure o' that?" Big Al demanded suspiciously.

"Sure. Jake and me came back to check and we could see the break in the ice where they went through. We even spotted some o' their gear floatin' downriver."

"Good! It's about time." Big Al sounded mollified by the news. "Those kids knew too much—and they were too smart to fool around with. They were makin' monkeys out of all you guys!"

"Aw, boss, we couldn't help it if—" The rest of Jake's whining protest was lost in the wind.

"Shut up!" Big Al roared. "One thing's sure— anything those kids knew, they've told their father. So he'll have to be the next one to go. Slip Gun, you're supposed to be handlin' things in town. You take care of Hardy tonight. Get me?"

"Yeah." Only a single word—and again too low for the voice to be identified.

Frank and Joe looked at each other, stunned. The gang had their father marked for death! They would *have* to return in time to warn him!

"The weather's gettin' worse all the time, boss," Slim put in. "How much longer do we have to keep searchin'?"

1

"Listen, you!" Big Al's voice was fierce. "I staked out that loot twenty-five years ago. And I aim to have it! We're goin' to keep lookin' till we find the wreck of a plane. The stuff'll be there, all right—and a skeleton with it."

"How do you know there's a wreck?" Jake asked.

"Don't worry—I made sure." Big Al gave an ugly chuckle. Again his rough voice drifted up to the listeners on the cliff. "Enough talkin'. Get these supply boxes cut open and load the horses. We'll leave part of the stores cached here and take the rest up to the hideout."

From below came the sound of cardboard boxes being ripped open, and the mumble of the men's voices. Suddenly Frank and Joe heard an exclamation of annoyance.

"What's wrong now?" Big Al snarled.

"Looks like Slip Gun just broke his knife blade," Jake replied.

Before the unidentified man could add anything, the gang leader snapped curtly, "Never mind gripin'! Use your fingers!"

Presently they could hear the men loading the horses. A few moments later the boys heard Big Al's harsh tones: "You've all had your orders. Now let's get goin'!"

Horses' hoofs started up on a rocky surface somewhere below—then faded bit by bit, echoing hollowly.

Joe grabbed his brother's arm. "There must be a passage from the canyon that leads out through the hill!" he whispered excitedly.

"Right! We'd better get back to the trail and see if we can spot them!"

Frank led the way as the brothers hurried back to the site from which they had first noticed the bearlike rock formation. Sprawling among the snow and rocks to avoid being seen, the Hardys gazed intently down the hillside.

For a long while there was no sign of humans. The sun had vanished behind clouds, leaving a leaden, wintry sky. Nothing was visible below but the vast, rugged expanse of timber-clad wilderness.

Joe fidgeted anxiously. "Those fellows can't just disappear!" he muttered. "They'll have to come out somewh—"

Frank held up his hand for silence. "There they are!" he whispered.

Far below and off to the right, four riders had emerged from a patch of brush on the hillside. They paused momentarily, then separated. Three of the men rode upward through a notch in the hills. The fourth headed off in the direction of Lucky Lode, leading an empty pack horse behind his mount.

"That one by himself must be Slip Gun!" Joe groaned. "If only we had binoculars to see who he is!"

"Maybe we can overtake him," Frank said hopefully. "Anyhow, the important thing is to get to the cabin and warn Dad. Let's go!"

Quickly the boys got their horses, swung into the saddles, and started off along the trail. They watched for a safe place to descend the hillside and soon picked out a likely route. The downslope, even here, was steep and slippery, but their horses managed to negotiate it successfully.

Minutes later, Frank and Joe picked up Slip Gun's trail in the snow. By this time the spy was far ahead and lost to view among the timber.

As the boys rode along, Joe fumed impatiently. "We'll lose him if we don't make better time!" he said, urging his horse to greater speed.

"Take it easy, Joe," Frank advised. "This ground is pretty rough going for the horses—they're doing the best they can. It won't help any if one of them breaks a leg."

Joe admitted the wisdom of his brother's words, and they pressed forward at the best pace they could manage.

"You know," Frank said, "I'm beginning to see why Hopkins was so interested when he saw Mike Onslow's map."

"You must be thinking the same thing I am," Joe returned. "Big Al must be looking for Onslow's missing gold!"

Frank pounded his fist into his palm as another thought struck him. "And, if he staked it out twenty-five years ago," he added excitedly, "that means—Big Al and Black Pepper are the same person! Also, the wrecked plane they're looking for must be the crate Bart Dawson took off in!"

Joe nodded thoughtfully. "Big Al seems to be sure Dawson died in the wreck."

"Which doesn't fit in with what Ben Tinker told us," Frank pointed out. "Ben claimed he saw Dawson in Helena a couple of years later."

"True—though nobody around here seems to believe anything Ben says."

"I know—but he *did* hear the music in the dance hall."

Joe chuckled. "That's right. Of course it wasn't exactly played by Charlie's ghost."

Dusk was gathering fast. By the time the boys had passed through the stretch of timber, it was no longer possible to make out Slip Gun's tracks, nor see the rider ahead. By now Frank and Joe were able to recognize familiar landmarks and inside of an hour were crossing the ridge above Lucky Lode. The town lights were visible below.

"It's tough luck we weren't able to nab Slip Gun," Frank said, as the brothers spurred their horses down the trail.

"Let's hope we're not too late to warn Dad!" Joe said grimly.

There was no sign of the horseman they were pursuing as they pounded through the streets of Lucky Lode. The boys' fears mounted when they drew in sight of Hank's cabin. Although darkness had fallen, no lights showed in the windows.

Frank and Joe reined to a halt, leaped from their horses, and dashed inside, fear gripping them.

"Hank! Dad!" Frank shouted.

No one answered. Without bothering to light the oil lamp, the boys blundered through the darkness and hastily checked the two sleeping rooms and the kitchen.

The cabin was empty!

·13·

A Fight in the Dark

"WE'RE too late!" Frank muttered in a choked voice.

Joe was too stunned to speak. The killer must have arrived before them! But where had the victims been taken?

The next instant the Hardys stiffened in suspense. Someone was slipping quietly into the cabin through the half-open front door.

"That you, boys?" It was Hank Shale!

Frank and Joe rushed to question him.

"What happened to Dad?" Joe exclaimed.

"Don't worry—your pa's safe," the Westerner assured them. "I just finished movin' him to Ben Tinker's place."

A wave of relief swept over the boys. "Did you know he was in danger?" Frank asked.

"We figgered so. After I told him how Big Al's men tried to get you lads, your pa had a hunch the gang might come after him next."

"His hunch was right," Joe said. "Big Al's spy was ordered to kill Dad tonight!"

Hank gave a low whistle. "By jingo, then he took cover just in time!" Hank listened tensely as the boys related their latest adventures.

"We'd better not wait any longer," Frank declared. "The killer may make his move any time now. Hank, you'd better go back to Ben's place and stand guard!"

"What about you two?"

"We'll wait here at the cabin and see if Slip Gun shows up," Frank replied.

"And if he does," Joe declared, "we'll catch him red-handed!"

"Now hold on!" said Hank. "If this feller's comin' to kill your pa, he'll be armed. It'd be plumb foolish to try takin' him on alone."

"Then we'll wait outside and just see who he is," Frank promised hastily. "The arrest can be handled later."

Hank started back to Ben Tinker's. Meanwhile, Joe lighted the oil lamp and the boys rummaged quickly through their father's gear for extra flashlights to replace the ones they had lost in the river. Then they extinguished the lamp and hurried outside.

After stabling their horses in the lean-to, without taking time to unsaddle them, the boys darted into a nearby clump of trees. They picked out a spot from which they could watch the front door of the cabin and waited. For the next quarter of an hour nothing disturbed the peaceful quiet of the icy night.

Suddenly Frank gave a low hiss and pointed towards the cabin. The boys could barely discern the figure of a man, moving silently. He tried the door cautiously, then slipped inside.

"Think we should try to nab him?" Joe whispered.

"We promised Hank we wouldn't," Frank reminded his brother. "But don't worry—once he comes back, we won't let him out of our sight till we've identified him. This time he won't give us the slip!"

The boys fell silent as a faint glow of light showed through the cabin window. The glow moved about. Evidently the intruder had brought a flashlight of his own.

The Hardys stiffened in surprise as a second figure suddenly loomed in the darkness near the cabin. The newcomer halted for an instant, then moved swiftly towards the door and went inside.

Joe gasped, "Two of them!"

A second later came a muffled outburst of voices, then a sharp cry. Confused noises followed, then a crash.

"They're fighting!" Frank sprang up. "Come on! That second person must have surprised the killer—he may need help!"

Joe followed as his brother sprinted from their hiding place. Frank reached the cabin first and tried to open the door. But it resisted his efforts, as if something were blocking it.

Frank braced his shoulder and slammed hard against the wood. This time it yielded and came open part way.

"Wait—wait a minute!" a voice just inside muttered thickly.

The boys pushed on through and almost stumbled over someone on the floor. Frank snapped on his flashlight. Its bright beam revealed the face of Burke, the storekeeper!

"Never mind me! Get him!" Burke rasped as he struggled to his feet. "He went through the back window!"

Joe had already switched on his flashlight. As Burke

spoke, the beam swept through the doorway and showed an open window.

Joe darted out the front door and ran to the back of the cabin. Frank dashed straight to the bedroom and stuck his head out the window.

Tracks were visible in the snow, leading off towards the heavy brush and timber skirting the hillside. Joe came around the corner of the cabin, picked out the footprints with the beam of his flashlight, and began following them.

"Hold it, Joe!" Frank called. "That fellow might have a gun!"

Joe halted unwillingly and looked back at his brother. "If he had a gun, wouldn't he have used it on Burke?"

"How do we know?" Frank argued. "Maybe he had no chance to draw before he knocked Burke down—and after he heard us at the door, he may have been more interested in making a getaway. Anyhow, don't risk it, Joe!"

"Okay." Joe shrugged and returned to the cabin.

By this time Burke was sitting down, and Frank had righted the overturned table and chairs. The store-keeper was dishevelled and had a raw-looking bruise on his right cheek.

"What happened?" Frank asked him.

"I came here to see you boys or your dad," Burke replied. "Instead, I discovered Bob Dodge nosin' around with a flashlight—"

"Dodge!" Frank and Joe exclaimed together.

"You heard me!" the storekeeper snapped. He rubbed his cheek gingerly. "I accused him of bein' a crook, and he slugged me with his flashlight. Then we started fightin'. Finally Dodge knocked me down against the door, and before I could get up, he scrammed."

"If Dodge had the flashlight, how could you see who he was?" Joe asked.

"I couldn't at first," Burke explained. "I called out, 'Who are you?' or 'Who's there?'—somethin' like that. Then he started givin' me some cock-and-bull story about lookin' for your dad and Hank Shale, and I recognized his voice. I said, 'Don't try to kid me, Dodge—you're in with that gang Mr Hardy's after!' That's when he conked me with the flashlight."

The boys looked at each other in bewilderment.

"What made you suspect Dodge is in league with Big Al's gang?" Frank questioned.

"Because I suddenly remembered him buyin' some red paint soon after your dad first came to Lucky Lode," Burke replied. "It slipped my mind when you boys asked me. That's what I was comin' here to tell you."

Frank and Joe digested this startling news. Burke's story added up to a convincing case against Dodge.

"That would explain why he fled," Joe said. "If he figured the game was up, Mr Dodge may have headed for the gang's hideout."

"Or taken off in his 'copter!" Frank exclaimed. "I'll see if it's still where he landed us."

"We'll both go," Joe said.

"No need for that," his brother argued. "You'd better help Mr Burke back to his store."

From the quick look his brother flashed him, Joe guessed that Frank still mistrusted Burke and wanted the man kept under surveillance.

Burke, however, declined the offer. "Don't worry about me," he said. "I'm okay now."

The storekeeper stood up to go, but after taking a few steps, he teetered and leaned weakly against the wall.

"Whew!" Burke muttered, shaking his head. "Guess I'm still a bit woozy from that clout Dodge gave me."

Joe helped him back to the chair, then went for some water from the kitchen pump. Before leaving, Frank made an excuse to join Joe.

"Take Burke to the store," he whispered. "Then go straight to Ben Tinker's and make sure Dad's okay. I'll meet you there."

Frank went outside, got his horse from the lean-to, and rode off towards the clearing where he judged the helicopter was parked.

Joe, meanwhile, bathed Burke's head with cold water and bandaged his injured cheek.

"Where did your dad go?" Burke asked.

"He and Hank Shale are following a lead on the case," Joe said vaguely. He then suggested that they take the remaining two horses and ride, rather than walk, to the store.

Burke shook his head. "It's not far enough to bother. Besides, the way I feel, I'm not sure I could stick on to a saddle."

Joe assisted him on foot to the store with no further difficulty. Burke thanked him, said good night, and went inside. Joe lingered until he saw the light go out. Then he hurried to Ben Tinker's cabin.

The young detective found Mr Hardy, Hank, and Ben awake and gathered around a glowing potbelly stove. They listened with keen interest as Joe poured out his story of the night's events. Just as he was finishing, there came the sound of a horse being reined up outside, and a moment later Frank burst into the cabin.

"The helicopter's still at the field," Frank reported. "I scouted around a bit, but there's no sign of Dodge. And he hasn't returned to the hotel."

Mr Hardy frowned and stroked his jaw. "I find it hard to believe that Bob Dodge can be a criminal—much less a killer," the detective said. "What's your opinion, boys?"

"Until tonight it seemed to me to be a toss up between Burke and Dodge," Joe replied. "We've suspected one of them must be Big Al's spy, ever since that night we trailed the hooded man to the general store."

Frank nodded and tallied up the evidence.

His father said, "Burke may be lying about what happened at the cabin tonight. Are you sure Dodge wasn't the second man to arrive?"

"It was too dark to tell," Frank admitted. "But you're right—Dodge may have surprised Burke there and accused *him* of working with the gang. And Burke may have done the attacking but got knocked down."

"In that case, why should Dodge duck out the window?" Hank objected.

"Burke was blocking the door," Joe said. "Maybe Dodge decided to get out fast, in case Burke came at him again."

Ben Tinker put in, "That still don't explain where he disappeared to."

Mr Hardy arose from his chair and paced back and forth. "The flashlight might carry fingerprints," he remarked. "Was it still around?"

"I didn't see it," Joe replied. "Dodge must have taken it with him."

"But we don't know that," Frank emphasized. "Burke could have slipped it inside his coat while we were looking out back."

Joe agreed. "We should have checked on that right away."

Frank suddenly snapped his fingers. "Let's assume Dodge is innocent. And if he got those burrs on his coat up at the cemetery, he must have been the *third* man— the one we heard behind us."

"Yes, and he may have spotted the blue signal light and gone to investigate just as we did."

"Right," Frank went on. "So maybe Dodge suspected all along that Burke was the man who met Slim. But he didn't want to jump to conclusions. Then, when he discovered Burke at the cabin tonight, he accused him outright—and Burke got panicky and jumped him."

Ben Tinker grunted suspiciously. "If Dodge suspected Burke, whyn't he tell you lads or your pa?"

"Matter of fact, Dodge did come around yesterday," Hank reminded them. "But the doc was tendin' to Fenton, and the boys weren't here, so he never got to talk to 'em."

"Maybe that's why Dodge came to the cabin tonight —to tell us his suspicions," Mr Hardy conjectured. "Has Burke ever been in trouble with the law?" he asked.

Hank and Ben replied that so far as they knew, he had not.

Frank began pacing the floor. "As things stand, we can make out a pretty convincing case *for* or *against* either Burke or Dodge," he stated. "Dodge has disappeared but Burke is still around. What we need is some way to test Burke's innocence—or guilt."

Mr Hardy nodded. "Good thinking."

"We know that the gang wants Joe and me out of the way," Frank went on. "And we also know they're after Mike Onslow's lost gold. So let's set a trap for Burke."

"How?" asked Joe.

Frank grinned and said coolly, "By using the best possible bait—the gold and ourselves!"

·14·

The Broken Knife

FRANK explained his plan while the others listened approvingly.

"Right smart idea, boy!" Ben Tinker cackled appreciatively. "If Burke's in league with the gang, I'll lay ten to one he snaps at the bait!"

Mr Hardy agreed. "But you boys should have a lawman on hand when the trap is sprung."

"I'll go along," Hank Shale volunteered. "And I'll get Sheriff Kenner over at Bear Creek."

After details of the planned capture had been settled, Mr Hardy said, "You boys had better bunk here for the night, if Ben will permit. It might be risky staying at Hank's place, in case the gang makes another attempt on our lives."

Ben willingly approved, and the boys said they would stretch out on blankets by the stove.

"We'll have to make one more trip back to Hank's, though, to tend the horses," Joe added.

The brothers set out, riding double on Frank's horse. By this hour the long, single street of Lucky Lode was dark and silent. When the Hardys reached Hank's cabin, they dismounted and went to the lean-to.

It was empty! Both Joe's horse and Daisy, the pack mare, were gone!

"Who could have taken them?" Joe gasped.

Frank was equally mystified. "Maybe footprints will give us a clue," he said hopefully.

The boys shone their flashlights around the trampled snow. Horseshoe prints led off up the hillside. A man's tracks were heading *towards* the cabin from the patch of timber into which Dodge had disappeared earlier.

"He must have come back after we left!" Joe exclaimed.

"Sure looks that way," Frank agreed. "We can check more carefully by daylight."

The boys returned to Ben's and stabled Frank's horse in one of the old ghost-town buildings. When they went inside the cabin, the three men were asleep. Ben was snoring loudly.

"Even *that* won't keep me awake tonight!" Joe grinned, and yawned deeply.

In spite of their exhausting adventures, Frank and Joe awoke at daybreak, thoroughly refreshed. After pulling on their clothes, they hurried back to Hank Shale's cabin.

Although the snow had wind-drifted, it was still possible to make out Dodge's tracks. They led away from the cabin to the woods, then returned to the lean-to.

"He was dazed, all right," Frank remarked. "His steps zigzagged."

The prints led to a clump of brush, where the crushed, broken twigs indicated the fugitive had fallen full length.

"Dodge collapsed when he got this far!" Joe said in surprise.

"Yes, Joe. And this may prove his innocence."

"How so?"

"Suppose it was Burke who hit *him* with the flashlight, instead of the other way around. Dodge might have fought back, knocked Burke down, then scrammed out the window before Burke could come at him again. Dodge may have been dazed from the blow—"

"I get it!" Joe interrupted excitedly. "So he staggered out here in the woods, maybe not even knowing where he was going, and passed out."

Frank said he was puzzled. "Why should Dodge go riding off up the hillside, instead of back into town? And why take Daisy?"

Joe shook his head. "Maybe we have him figured all wrong. Could be he *is* part of the gang, and wanted to get up to their hideout."

Frank and Joe checked again on the helicopter and found it still in the clearing. On their way back through Lucky Lode, the Hardys stopped off at the hotel. The worried manager informed them that he had had no word from the vanished armoured-car-company owner.

"I've notified Sheriff Kenner and I just now finished calling Mr Dodge's office in Helena," the manager added.

Back at Ben's cabin, the boys found a hearty breakfast awaiting them. As they ate, Frank and Joe reported the theft of the two horses and discussed their theories with the men.

"An amazing turn of events," Mr Hardy said.

As soon as the meal was over, Hank and the boys went off to hire fresh mounts from the livery stable.

They promised to pay the owner for the lost horse if it was not recovered. Hank started off for Bear Creek to meet the sheriff. Meanwhile, Frank and Joe rode to the general store.

"Mornin', boys," Burke greeted them. Aside from his bruised cheek, he seemed to have suffered no ill effects from the fight.

Frank read off a short list of supplies. One item was a box of canned beans. When Burke brought it, Frank said, "We'd better divide the cans between our saddle-bags, Joe. Could you lend me a knife to open the box, Mr Burke?"

"Sure," Burke took out a huge pocketknife and tossed it on to the counter.

As the storekeeper went off to get the rest of the items, Frank opened the knife. About half the main blade was broken off!

The Hardys exchanged quick glances of triumph. The first part of Frank's plan had paid off. Unless the broken knife was an amazing coincidence, Burke must be the man the gang called "Slip Gun"! Now to see if he would take the bait they were about to offer!

As Frank had hoped, Burke was curious as to why the boys needed the supplies. "You fellas fixin' to take a trip somewhere?" he asked casually as he totalled the bill.

"Not too far," Frank replied. "We'll be camping in a canyon up the mountain a ways."

"And we'll be coming back rich!" Joe added boastfully.

Frank shot an angry look at his brother, as if Joe had spoken out of turn.

"Rich?" Burke looked at the boys questioningly.

"It was supposed to be a secret," Frank grumbled, "but—well, I guess we can trust you after what happened last night."

"Sure! I won't tell nobody," Burke purred.

"Well, one reason we came out West was to look for some lost gold that an old miner named Mike Onslow told us about," Frank began.

"He drew us a map," put in Joe, "but it was stolen from us."

"Then yesterday we were out in a box canyon where there's a certain rock formation that looks like a bear," Frank went on. "We'd heard Big Al's gang planned to meet there. We didn't see the gang, but we did spot a clue to the whereabouts of the gold. And we have the location marked right here on a map we drew ourselves."

Frank pulled a folded piece of paper from his pocket and tapped it significantly.

Burke stared in amazement. "No foolin'! You really know where to lay hands on the gold?"

The boys nodded gloatingly.

"But please don't say a word to anyone," Joe cautioned. "We don't want to start a gold rush out to that canyon before we've had a chance to uncover the treasure."

"Don't worry, boys! Mum's the word as far as I'm concerned." Burke gave an oily smile.

After stowing the supplies in their saddlebags, Frank and Joe rode out of town. Beyond the ridge they reined up at a sheltered spot agreed upon beforehand with Hank. Here the boys waited until they were joined by Hank and Sheriff Kenner. Then all four set out together, retracing the route the Hardys had followed when returning to town from the canyon the evening before.

A brief search soon disclosed the opening in the hillside through which the gang had emerged from the canyon. The entrance widened into a high-arched rocky passage, big enough for riding two abreast. The passage ended directly below the bear-shaped rock.

Once inside, Frank, Joe, and their two companions paused to consider their next move.

Sheriff Kenner, a rugged-looking man with an iron-grey moustache, asked the boys, "What time do you figure the gang will show—assuming Burke took the bait?"

"He jumped at it!" Joe declared confidently.

"My hunch is," Frank said, "they'll wait until after dark and try to take us by surprise."

The group kept out of sight below the rocky overhang and Hank cooked lunch over a small fire. Meanwhile, the two boys searched for the broken knife blade. Joe soon found it.

"This sure looks as if it fits Burke's knife," he said, handing over the blade to the sheriff.

By the time darkness fell, the group had arranged a convincing-looking camp with two stone-and-brush dummies covered with blankets to resemble sleepers. Then the four retired with their horses behind a cluster of huge boulders.

Time passed slowly. The campfire was renewed. Suddenly, above the soughing of the wind, the listeners' ears caught the faint clop of horses' hoofs. The riders were coming through the rocky passage. Frank, Joe, and their two companions swung quietly into their saddles. Sheriff Kenner whispered final orders.

Moments later, three horsemen entered the canyon. There was sufficient moonlight for the boys to make out Slim and Jake. The third man, they guessed, was Big Al. Evidently Burke was not taking part in the raid.

The three thugs paused inside the canyon. The dying campfire and the two blanketed dummies lay in plain view. Big Al hissed out an order. Slim and Jake charged forward, their horses breaking into a gallop. The gang leader followed at a more leisurely pace.

"All right, let's take 'em!" Sheriff Kenner snapped in a low voice. He and Hank spurred their horses from behind the boulders, while Frank and Joe waited, according to plan.

"Don't go for your guns! Just reach!" Sheriff Kenner yelled. At the same time, he fired a shot to show that he meant business.

Slim and Jake reined up sharply. Their hands shot skyward in panic as the bullet whistled over their heads. Frank and Joe spurred their horses into action and sped from behind the boulders. At that same instant Big Al wheeled his horse in a wild dash for the passageway. The boys and Hank followed, but suddenly Hank's horse stumbled and its rider went flying off. The Hardys stopped, and turned back to help him.

"I'll—be all right—boys. Nothin'—broken! Just— got the—wind knocked out o' me," he called out.

Reassured, Joe swung his mount in the direction of the escaping outlaw. "Big Al's getting away! Let's go after him!" he called to his brother.

Frank needed no urging. Together, they galloped

after the ringleader. With Slim and Jake to deal with, the sheriff was powerless to join the chase. He shouted a warning to the two boys, advising them to wait, but his cry was drowned by the thundering hoofbeats.

The boys were already plunging through the tunnel in hot pursuit of the outlaw. In the darkness ahead they could hear the pounding hoofs of Big Al's mount and see an occasional glint of sparks as its steel shoes struck the rocks.

Presently a dim glow of moonlight showed the passageway coming to an end. For a time Big Al's figure was clearly silhouetted. Then it was lost to view as he emerged from the passage and headed to the right along the foot of the hillside. In moments Frank and Joe were out of the passageway and turning their own horses in the same direction.

"Big Al's heading towards the same notch he and his men aimed for yesterday!" Frank called.

For more than an hour the chase continued—over rocks, through dangerous gullies, then along a river winding through a narrow canyon. Suddenly Frank and Joe lost sight of their quarry as the canyon curved sharply. When the boys rounded the bend, they reined up in astonishment.

Ahead, the canyon ended abruptly in a high frozen cataract. The outlaw had vanished!

·15·

Underground Chase

FRANK and Joe looked at each other in sheer disbelief, mingled with uneasiness. Except for the panting of their horses, not a sound broke the wintry silence of the canyon.

"Could Big Al have rigged some kind of ambush?" Joe asked in a low, worried voice.

"I don't see how," Frank murmured, scanning the terrain. "There's no place for him and his horse to hide."

The cliff walls on either side were bare and precipitous. With the moon almost directly overhead, the snow-covered floor of the canyon was revealed with brilliant clarity. The narrow riverbanks were barren of brush. Aside from a few scattered rocks—none big enough to afford cover—nothing intervened between the boys and the frozen waterfall.

"Well, he must be here somewhere," Joe said edgily. "His tracks will give us the answer."

Frank agreed. The boys dismounted and moved forward cautiously, leading their horses. Moonlight wrapped the scene in eerie loneliness. The boys kept their eyes and ears alert. Gradually they became aware of another sound—the muted roar of falling water, still flowing behind the glacier-like formation.

The sound became louder as they neared the cataract. The majestic ice curtain glittered in the moonlight. It was fringed with great, jagged blue-white spears that hung down like stalactites.

"I don't get it," Joe muttered. "Al's tracks lead straight towards the waterfall!"

As they proceeded, Frank took out his flashlight, and switched it on. He gave a cry of surprise.

"Joe! He must have gone *under* the waterfall!"

At the base of the cliff was a dark open space yawning between the curve of the falls and the rock face! It was large enough to admit a horse and rider. The boys moved closer for a better look and Frank probed the darkness with his flashlight.

"Look! There's an opening in the cliff wall!" Joe exclaimed. "It must be a tunnel!"

"Or maybe just a blind cavern," Frank said, switching off his flashlight. "Big Al could be waiting for us in there!"

After a whispered conference, Frank groped his way behind the cataract. When he reached the opening in the cliff he quickly snapped on his flashlight again for a more leisurely examination.

Presently he came back and reported to Joe. "It's a tunnel, all right. No telling how far it goes—or where."

"No sign of Big Al?" Joe questioned.

"Not in person, but there are wet tracks."

The two horses balked a bit as the boys took their bridles and attempted to lead them into the dark space behind the icy falls. Joe's animal, which was in the lead, whinnied and reared when it felt the splattering spray, but it soon calmed under Joe's reassuring hand.

Inside the tunnel mouth the passage widened, giving the boys room to mount. Frank and Joe rode slowly forward, with Joe, in the lead, shining his flashlight.

After several hundred yards the passage widened and the boys were able to ride side by side.

"Must have been the bed of an old underground stream," Frank guessed. "See how smooth the walls are worn."

Joe nodded. "We'd better speed up before Big Al gets too far ahead."

Urging their horses to a faster pace, they pushed on through the tunnel. At intervals the boys stopped and listened, hoping to catch some sound of their quarry. The fourth time they halted, a faint echoing sound of horse's hoofs on rock reached their ears from somewhere ahead.

"We must be getting closer!" Joe said tensely.

Just how close was difficult to judge, since the enclosed passage with its smooth, hard walls might carry the sound almost any distance. The boys rode on steadily. When they paused to listen once more, the hoofbeats were no longer audible. But twenty minutes later Joe thought he could detect them again.

"He may be far ahead of us," said Frank. "Sound can be pretty tricky in here."

As the brothers continued along the tunnel, the chill, dank atmosphere gradually became warmer. Frank and Joe unzipped their heavy jackets.

After a while it became necessary to rest the horses. The Hardys did not dare pause too long for fear of losing Big Al completely, and soon went on.

The tunnel turned and twisted. The horses were

nervous at first about proceeding, but gradually became accustomed to the experience.

"It seems as if we've been travelling for hours," said Frank. Presently he snapped on his flashlight to glance at his wristwatch. To his amazement, it was almost three-thirty in the morning! "Whew! Do you realize the night's almost over, Joe?"

"I sure do. The horses are bushed."

Gradually the boys became aware that the tunnel was sloping upward. The horses began to pant and labour from the steepness of the incline, and the Hardys had to rest them more frequently.

"It's getting colder in here," Joe said with a sudden shiver. Both boys zipped up their jackets.

"We must be getting close to the surface," Frank said hopefully.

Sometime later he was about to turn on his flashlight again when he paused. "Hey! The tunnel's not so dark as it has been—or am I imagining things?"

"You're right!" Joe replied, with rising excitement. "I'll keep my flashlight off for a while."

Soon the boys could feel cold air on their faces. The tunnel was lightening every moment, and presently a grey glimmer of daylight showed ahead. With joyful cries of relief, Frank and Joe urged their horses forward.

In a minute or so, they had emerged on to a snow-covered mountainside. Rocks, scattered trees, and slopes all around them were bathed in the ghostly light of dawn. The Hardys leaped from their horses, stretched their tired muscles, and inhaled the fresh air deeply. Then they looked around and assessed their situation.

"There are Big Al's tracks," Joe said, pointing them out.

Frank nodded. "Fairly fresh, too—but he could be a good distance ahead of us."

"Any idea where we are, Frank?"

"Not much, except that we've come clear through the mountain." Frank grinned wryly. "I'm famished, Joe. How about you?"

"Same here! Think we can take time to eat?"

"May as well," Frank decided. "No telling how long we'll be on the trail. Lucky we didn't unpack."

The boys fed their horses, built a small fire, and had breakfast. Then they swung back into the saddles and resumed their pursuit of the outlaw. His tracks led upwards on to a beaten trail winding along the mountainside.

When they reached the path, Frank reined in his mount and glanced towards a high, jutting rock formation farther up the mountain. "Know something, Joe?" he remarked. "I'll bet this is a continuation of Ambush Trail."

Joe snapped his fingers. "You're right! I remember seeing that rocky outcrop way in the distance, just before we fell into the river!"

"If this *is* Ambush Trail," Frank went on, "Big Al must be heading for their hideout on Windy Peak."

"That figures," Joe agreed. "He thinks he's shaken us by going through the tunnel."

The boys continued their pursuit throughout the morning. Around midday, Big Al's tracks left the well-defined path and disappeared upward among the higher rocks and brush.

Joe groaned at the sight. "Good grief! How can we tackle that kind of ground when our horses are exhausted already?"

Frank looked thoughtful as they slouched in their saddles and studied the terrain. "Maybe there's no need to, Joe. I have a hunch this could be a dodge to throw us off."

"You could be right," Joe said, brightening. "If Big Al's heading for Windy Peak, he'll probably *have* to come back to the trail eventually."

After talking the matter over, the Hardys decided to halt for lunch and a rest. Two hours later, feeling refreshed, they hit the trail again.

It was late in the afternoon when the boys sighted the outlaw's tracks once more, leading from the slope back down to the trail.

"Your hunch paid off, Frank!" Joe exclaimed. "These tracks look pretty fresh, too!"

Encouraged, the boys pressed forward with new energy. A mile farther on, the trail forked. One branch struck sharply upward. The other followed a more winding course along the curve of the mountainside. To their left stretched a shallow box canyon.

Frank and Joe took the lower trail, since the prints showed that Big Al had gone that way. Gradually the path became little more than a rocky ledge, with frequent sharp turns and a sheer drop-off along the outer edge. The Hardys rode single file, with Joe in the lead.

Suddenly a pebble clattered down from a rock jutting out just above their heads. Frank shot a quick glance upward. "Look out, Joe!" he yelled.

A rope with a wide circling noose was snaking down towards his brother's head!

Frank's warning came an instant too late. The noose settled over Joe's shoulders and jerked tight, nearly yanking him from the saddle.

Frank spurred forward, white with terror. Someone hidden on the ledge above them was trying to drop Joe over the precipice! Frank managed to grab the taut rope just in time. Almost at the same instant, the unseen enemy let go of it. Joe would have gone over the brink, but Frank's quick jerk on the rope pulled his brother back from the edge, and Joe dropped heavily on to the trail. Unhurt, he struggled to his feet and began extricating himself from the noose. In moments he was free.

"There goes the rat!" Frank yelled as a figure burst from the ledge above and scrambled rapidly along the slope.

Big Al!

Instantly Joe was back in the saddle. The Hardys spurred forward in hot pursuit. The outlaw's course was roughly parallel to the trail. Suddenly Big Al checked his stride long enough to send a large rock rumbling down the slope.

"Hold it, Frank!" Joe warned.

Both boys yanked their horses to a rearing, whinnying halt in the nick of time! A split second later the rock crashed on to the trail just ahead, rolled to the edge, and went over.

The animals snorted with fear and stood trembling. Frank and Joe barely managed to spur them into motion again. Big Al was lost to view behind a clump of brush and jagged outcropping.

The trail ahead bent sharply around a projecting shoulder of the mountainside. Joe caught a quick glimpse of Big Al outlined against the sky as he rounded the slope. Then he disappeared.

The boys slowed their mounts to negotiate the dangerous hairpin curve of the ledge. As they came around to the opposite side of the shoulder, Joe reined in and signalled Frank to halt. Ahead stood Big Al's riderless horse. The Hardys dismounted to scout the situation.

"Where has he gone?" Frank asked tensely.

"Search me," Joe replied, looking around.

Just past the outlaw's horse the trail petered out and the terrain sloped upward in a jumble of giant rocks. Beyond them a huge boulder stood poised straight up like a pinnacle.

"He must be holed up among those rocks," Frank said. "Probably waiting for us!"

He had hardly finished speaking when Joe clutched his brother's arm and pointed. "Look! There he is!"

Big Al had suddenly appeared, clawing his way to the very top of the jutting boulder!

"He's trapped!" Frank cried out triumphantly. "Let's get him!"

Cliff Hideaway

"YOU'LL never take me alive!" screamed Big Al.

He had reached the top of the huge boulder and now stood waving his arms against the leaden sky. The outlaw was jumping around as though half-crazed.

"Try to get me!" he challenged.

As Frank and Joe sped into the jumble of rocks, they lost sight of their quarry momentarily. They could hear Big Al still yelling, then suddenly there was silence.

"Wonder what happened?" Joe panted. "Did—"

He was interrupted by a long-drawn-out scream which gradually trailed off. Then there was silence.

Dashing from the rocks, the boys came around a corner. Before them was the huge boulder.

"He's gone!" Joe panted.

"But where?"

There was no place for Big Al to have run except down the rocky trail on which the boys had been.

"He must have jumped over the edge!" Joe yelled. The Hardys ran to it. They could see most of the canyon floor below them. There was no sign of a body.

"He *must* have gone down!" Frank said, puzzled. "But where is he?"

The boys looked closely again in the waning light. There was no one in sight.

"I wonder—" Joe said slowly. "Even if Big Al did go over the side, he may have known a safe way to slide to the bottom, and there might be some hiding place—"

Frank agreed. "Big Al's pretty tricky. He could have figured out some way to escape."

As the light failed, the brothers strained their eyes to peer into the darkness, but could detect no niche, crevice, or cave in which to hide.

"Well," Frank murmured at last, "there isn't much we can do tonight. I sure hate to think Big Al is roaming around here loose."

Joe looked towards the sky. It was dark now and they were a long distance up Windy Peak. "What'll we do, Frank?" he asked.

"The only thing we can do," said his brother, "is spend the night here. Tomorrow we might manage to find some trace of Big Al. I want to know if he's dead or alive."

"I do, too!" Joe exclaimed.

"We'll have to make camp," Frank said, "but first we'd better do something about our horses."

"Yes, and Big Al's, too," Joe added, pointing towards the outlaw's fine roan that was still ground-hitched.

The boys gathered the three animals together, rode back to the fork, and secured the horses to rocks.

"These old fellows will provide us with a good warning system," Frank remarked.

"How?" his brother asked.

Frank explained his idea. "We'll leave them here and go part way back along the trail to make camp. If Al is alive he'll *have* to come past here, since all three trails meet at this spot. He'll want his roan, anyway. The horses would be sure to whinny and waken us."

"Good scheme!" said Joe. "We'll camp at the Rock Motel!"

"Every comfort and all for free," Frank joked.

The boys ate, fed the horses, then carted their bedrolls and meagre supplies to a sheltered spot and quickly spread out the blankets. Though the brothers were tired, sleep was slow in coming.

"I can't help wondering if Big Al is tricking us again," Frank said uneasily as he was finally drifting off.

He dreamed several times about the outlaw and tried to figure out why he and Joe had not seen Big Al's body in the gorge. Both boys slept fitfully through the night.

As the blackness of the sky began to lighten with the coming of dawn, they got up and ate a cold but nourishing breakfast of oranges, oatmeal biscuits, and egg flakes. Refreshed, the boys walked towards the edge of the cliff over which Big Al had disappeared.

"We may be able to see something more in the daylight," Joe remarked.

Frank had been staring into the grey, lowering sky. "I doubt if there's anything to see," he observed.

"What do you mean?"

Frank scanned the sky once more. "I think we've been fooled again," he answered. "If there had been a body down in the gorge, there'd be carrion birds flying around."

"Of course," said Joe.

"I wondered about it last night, but thought maybe because it was so late there wouldn't be any birds at work. But some would be here this morning, if there was anything to attract them."

"Let's look over the edge again," Joe suggested.

The brothers dropped to their stomachs and crept as close as they could to the rim. By leaning well over it, they could look almost to the base of the cliff.

"See anything, Joe?"

"Not a thing."

Suddenly, from far below, came the rattle of small pebbles. A great black raven flew out of the precipice.

"There must be a nest in the cliff!" Joe cried out.

The boys edged forward over the rough stones. They held on as tightly as possible before leaning over to locate the nest.

"There it is!" exclaimed Frank.

Below them in a recess that nature had torn in the cliffside was the bird's nest and alongside it enough room to give a man shelter.

"That was Big Al's hiding place!" Frank said grimly. "He swung down there to the left and probably got away during the night."

Frank and Joe crawled back from the cliff's edge until they could stand up in safety.

"He fooled us all right," said Frank. "I wonder how long it was before he left here."

"Maybe," Joe suggested, "it depended on the horses. I'll bet he waited until just before dawn and then stole them!"

Frank was angry. "Of course. His horse would know him, and since the three animals have been together and become friends, none of them would whinny an alarm. I should have realized that."

The boys dashed for the fork. Their guess had been

right! The horses were gone! And taken up the steeper branch of the road!

"Al *did* trick us!" Frank chided himself.

"Now he's really got us in a spot," murmured his brother. "Do we head for home or trail him?"

"Trail him," Frank decided promptly. "We'll have to walk, of course."

"Can we make it up there?" Joe sounded worried.

"I don't know, but we'll have to try."

The brothers huddled in the shelter of a rock to discuss the situation. What lay ahead? They realized it might be a long and treacherous climb—perhaps another night without hot food and proper shelter. They noticed it was growing colder and that was a bad sign too. It was not only going to be uncomfortable for the Hardy boys, but they could easily freeze to death!

"Come on, Joe!" Frank said resolutely as he started up the steep trail. "We're not going to let Big Al get away!"

Joe joined his brother and together they started the climb along this part of Ambush Trail. The turns were abrupt and the wind whistled sharply. Once Joe had to snatch Frank back when the wind nearly blew him over the edge.

For hours the boys toiled along the trail, following the string of horseshoe prints. During the afternoon, the marks made an abrupt turn that opened on to a plateau. It was almost completely surrounded by jagged outcroppings of rocks. The boys ducked down out of the strong wind which had swept the area almost clean of snow.

Suddenly their eyes bulged as they spotted a small

cabin that lay nestled in the centre of the little plateau!
From its chimney came a thin wisp of smoke.

"Somebody's here!" said Joe excitedly, and instinctively began to run.

"Wait!" Frank warned. "It might be Big Al. We'd
better approach cautiously. Say, Joe—look!"

On a ridge beyond the cabin was a single weather-
beaten pine tree.

"The lone tree!" Joe exclaimed.

"Yes," said Frank, "and if it is, that building might
be Mike Onslow's cabin—now occupied by Big Al!"

· 17 ·

The Secret Listener

As the boys paused uncertainly, pondering their next move, the cabin door opened. A tall, white-haired man strode out and waved to them.

"Hi there!" he called. "Looking for shelter?"

The boys gasped as they recognized him.

"It's Mr Dodge!" Joe exclaimed.

"Can we trust him?" Frank muttered. "If he *is* in cahoots with the gang, Big Al may be in there, waiting to jump us."

Joe shot his brother a quick glance. "If we run for it, they may come after us shooting!"

"Guess we'll have to play this by ear," Frank said in a low voice. "Better pretend we don't suspect anything —but be ready to act fast if we spot a trap."

The Hardys walked towards the cabin.

"What are you doing up here, Mr Dodge?" Joe asked when they drew closer.

A bewildered look came over the man's face. "Dodge?" he repeated. "My name is Dawson—Bart Dawson. I worked a claim up here with Mike Onslow and the Coulson brothers."

The boys stopped short in astonishment.

"That's right," Dodge went on. His manner seemed

strange. "I—I'd better explain," he added. "Come on inside and I'll tell you the whole story. Maybe you boys can help me."

Frank and Joe looked at each other. Both had a hunch as to what Dodge was about to tell them.

"Okay, let's go," Frank murmured to Joe.

The brothers entered and Dodge closed the door. The cabin had a "lived-in" appearance. There were cans of food and other supplies on the shelves, and a pile of firewood beside the pot-belly stove.

"Sit down, boys."

Frank and Joe found chairs, but Dodge remained standing. He sighed and ran his fingers through his thick shock of white hair, as if he scarcely knew how to begin. He had a livid, swollen bruise on his right temple.

"Can you lads imagine what it's like to wake up suddenly and not know where you are or how you got there?" the big man said at last. "To have a complete blank in your memory?"

"A blank twenty-five years long?" Joe put in.

Dodge looked startled. "I don't know how you guessed it, son, but you must be just about right. Last time I recall, I was a young man with red hair and a beard. Also I was very skinny. But now when I see myself"—he gestured towards a small cracked mirror—"my hair's white, I'm years older, and I'm much heavier."

"Do you recognize us?" Frank queried.

The man shook his head. "No—and I've been wondering why you called me Dodge."

"Because you've been going under the name of Bob Dodge," Frank replied.

"Same initials—B.D.—but a different identity," Joe added.

After introducing himself and his brother, Frank went on, "You spoke about waking up suddenly. Where?"

"In some woods near a cabin," the man answered. "Felt as if I'd hit my head—or *been* hit—and there was a big swelling on my temple. Do you fellows know what happened?"

"You were conked with a flashlight," Joe told him.

Frank leaned forward and asked, "Can't you remember anything about a fight inside a cabin?"

Bart Dawson frowned in deep thought. Finally he shook his head. "No. I tried to figure how I'd got to the woods, but nothing came back to me."

"What did you do next?" Frank said.

"Well, I staggered out of the woods. It was dark, but I was close to someone's cabin. I knocked on the door, but—no answer."

"Is that any reason to steal two horses?" Joe asked accusingly.

Dawson flushed. "You seem to know all my actions. I guess it was pretty highhanded, helping myself like that. But believe me, I intended to bring them back."

"Just why did you take them?" Frank asked. "If you were confused, you could have gone into town for help."

"I guess so," Dawson admitted. "But the main street was dark and no one seemed to be stirring. Besides, I—well, I'd have felt pretty foolish waking people up and confessing I was mixed up.

"All I knew," the man went on, "was that my name was Bart Dawson and I had to find my partners fast.

It seemed terribly urgent for me to get back up here to our cabin on Windy Peak. There were two horses in the stable, so I helped myself to 'em and hit the trail. I took the pack horse," he added, "because it was carrying blankets and a few supplies which I figured I might need in case I got lost and had to camp in the open."

"When did you arrive here?" Frank asked.

"Yesterday afternoon. The place was empty, but there was some food."

Frank and Joe concluded this was the gang's hideout.

"When I saw myself in the mirror," Dawson went on, "I realized how many years must have gone by." His voice broke. He slumped down on a bunk and put his head in his hands. "If you boys can fill me in at all," he said, "I'd sure appreciate it."

Frank and Joe explained to Dawson that under the name Dodge, he had been operating a successful armoured-car business in Helena for ten years. Where he had been before that, they did not know. The boys also told him how he had engaged their father, Fenton Hardy, to run down a gang of robbers and how his sons had been brought into the case. Frank ended by telling Dawson about his fight with Burke at Hank Shale's cabin, and how a trap had been baited for Burke later, which resulted in the capture of Slim and Jake.

The white-haired man on the bunk shook his head hopelessly. "Thanks for telling me this, boys. But I still can't remember a thing about my life as Bob Dodge."

"What's the last thing you do remember?" Joe pressed him.

Slowly Dawson began to relate how he and his

partners had been besieged in this very cabin by Black Pepper's gang.

"We heard about that from Mike Onslow," Frank put in. "He's a trapper now, back East. The two Coulson brothers are dead."

Dawson swallowed hard. "I'm sorry to hear that." After a moment he continued, "Anyhow, I remember taking off in the plane and heading north. But after three or four minutes the engine failed—and the ship crashed."

"You couldn't have gone far in three or four minutes," Joe said thoughtfully.

"No, that's right," Dawson agreed, frowning. "I think I came down in the big valley beyond Lone Tree Ridge."

"Then what?" Frank asked.

Dawson got up from the bunk and paced back and forth. "The plane hit hard and cartwheeled over into a sort of little gully somewhere along the valley floor. I must have blacked out for a while. When I came to, I had a terrible pain in my head."

"You walked away from the wreck?" asked Joe.

"Yes. I was worried about Black Pepper getting the gold and the fact that Mike Onslow and the Coulson boys had entrusted it to me. Don't know how I managed, weak as I was, but somehow I got the sacks of gold out of the plane."

"What did you intend to do?" Frank inquired.

Dawson rubbed his head painfully. "I've been concentrating on that ever since I arrived at the cabin," he replied. "I recall knowing I couldn't lug the gold very far, and that I wanted to hide it in a safe place.

Some landmark in the valley must have reminded me of an old abandoned mine called the Lone Tree diggings."

"Is that where you took the gold?" Joe asked.

"It must have been," Dawson said. "Anyhow, I remember finding a tunnel opening—and at the end of the tunnel a big excavation with bluish dirt walls. That's where I hid the gold."

"Can you remember anything more?" Frank urged.

"Not much. Guess I tried to reach help. But it was bitter cold and snowing and I must have lost my way. Seems as if I wandered for a long time—plodding along blindly, falling, getting up, and staggering on. After that, everything's a blank."

"The crash and the terrible hardships you went through must have brought on amnesia," Joe said.

"And the blow Burke gave you that night triggered your mind into recalling the past," Frank added.

"Incidentally," Joe put in, "we're pretty sure that Black Pepper and the gang leader Big Al are the same man."

Dawson frowned again. "You said I was running a business up in Helena," he murmured. "In that case, why was I hanging around Lucky Lode? Your father was handling the detective work."

"We wondered about that ourselves," Frank admitted. "In fact, it made us suspect that you might be in with the gang. But maybe you were trying to dig up your past. I have a hunch this territory around Lucky Lode could have rung a bell in your mind."

Suddenly all three were startled by the whinny of a horse. Frank and Joe leaped from their chairs and dashed outside, followed by Dawson. A man on horse-back had just emerged from a clump of rocks and brush. He was headed towards the ridge.

"That's Big Al!" Joe cried.

A thought flashed into Frank's mind. Around the windward sides of the cabin lay an area of drift snow. Frank ran towards it. As he had feared, fresh tracks were visible leading towards and away from the lean-to shed at the back.

"He was here!" Frank called angrily. As the others joined him, he pointed to the prints in the snow. "I'll bet Big Al was hiding in the shed! He must have heard everything!"

The Hardys and Dawson hurried into the shed. Joe's saddle horse and Daisy, the pack mare—the animals Dawson had taken from Hank's cabin—were peacefully munching hay at the feedbox. Dawson was mystified, but Frank and Joe quickly reconstructed what must have happened.

"The gang's been using this cabin as their hideout," Joe said. "Big Al must have reached here just before we did. When he saw the smoke, Big Al figured he'd better scout the situation."

"Right," Frank agreed. "He circled around the cabin towards that clump of brush, left the horses there, and sneaked up from the rear."

"I'll bet he was in the lean-to when we arrived," Joe added. "That means he heard everything through the wall—including what Mr Dodge—Dawson—told us about the place where he hid the gold!"

"And now Big Al's on his way to find it!" Frank exclaimed.

The Hardys ran towards the clump of rocks and brush. Among them, well out of sight of the cabin, were the two horses Big Al had stolen from the boys. The outlaw had abandoned the extra animals when he galloped off.

"We'll go after him!" Frank decided.

The boys rode the horses back to the cabin. Dawson was eager to accompany them in pursuit of the gang leader, but the Hardys thought it more important that he return to Lucky Lode immediately and tell their father the turn of events.

"Dad and Hank and the sheriff will be worried sick about us by this time," Frank said. "Besides, Mr Dawson, that knock on the head may cause some after-effects—you should see a doctor."

After some persuasion, Dawson agreed, although the leaden sky indicated that bad weather was on its way.

Frank and Joe quickly collected some supplies from among the provisions in the cabin. In doing so, they discovered a powerful flashlight with a blue lens—evidently the signal light beamed from the cemetery—and a complete list of the gang members, with jotted notes on how to contact them, including Hopkins' group in Chicago.

"This should give the police all they need to smash the gang for good!" Joe exclaimed, handing the papers to Dawson.

Snow was falling as the boys mounted their horses. Dawson was ready to hit the trail for Lucky Lode with the other horses. After a final farewell Frank and Joe galloped off.

The snow was gradually obliterating Big Al's tracks.

By the time the Hardys had topped the ridge and were riding down into the valley below, the outlaw's trail had disappeared.

"A tough break," Frank murmured, "but at least we know the general direction he's taking."

An hour later they reached level ground. The sky was heavily overcast now and wind was roaring down the valley at gale force. The brothers hunched low in the saddle as driving gusts of snow stung their faces.

Frank took the lead while the boys threaded their way among boulders and brush that studded the valley floor. Here and there drifts were accumulating and the horses' legs sank deep into the snow at every step. Soon the snow was swirling so thickly that Frank could see only a few yards ahead. Had they made a mistake, he wondered, in pressing ahead through the storm?

"Looks as though we're in for a real blizzard, Joe!" he yelled. "We'd better find shelter!"

Hearing no answer, Frank swung around in the saddle—then gasped. Joe was nowhere in sight!

"Joe!" Frank screamed against the wind. "Joe! Where are you?"

There was no reply.

·18·

North from Lone Tree

For a moment Frank was panic-stricken. He shouted Joe's name, but the howling wind drowned his voice.

Snuggling his chin inside his turned-up coat collar, Frank slouched in his saddle and waited. Minutes dragged by. Again and again he called his brother's name, but no answering cry reached his ears. Darkness was closing in rapidly now, and Frank was half numbed from the icy blast of the storm. His heart sank with every passing moment.

"It's hopeless," Frank decided at last. "If I sit here much longer, I'll freeze. I must get out of the driving wind and snow." Frank urged his horse in the general direction of the mountainside.

Presently through the swirling snow, a shapeless, rocky mass loomed in front of him. Frank guided his horse along the base of the rock, and after several minutes of plodding, found a spot that was partially sheltered by overhang. He dismounted and drew his horse in out of the blizzard.

Frank clicked on his flashlight and shone it about the area. Fringing the rock face were brownish clumps of brush—dry and brittle beneath their coating of snow.

"These will do for a fire," Frank thought. "And it might signal Joe!"

He broke off enough of the brush to make a small pile and took out his waterproof case of matches. He struck one, then a second. Both blew out, but the third one caught. Cupping the flame in his hand, Frank held it against one of the broken twigs. In a moment the dry wood began to smoulder. Bit by bit, Frank nursed the ember into a fire and soon had a roaring blaze going.

"It won't last long, though," he reflected as he warmed his face and hands.

By now the circle of firelight was strong enough to reveal a fallen tree several yards away. Frank managed to break off some branches and brought them back to augment his supply of firewood.

"If only Joe was here!" he thought.

Shivering, Frank walked out into the darkness. "Joe!" he shouted, his voice straining. Then again, "Joe! . . ."

Frank listened intently. Suddenly his heart leaped. He had heard a cry!

Frank began yelling frantically. Several moments later a horse and rider took shape out of the snowy darkness. Frank rushed to meet them and guided Joe's frost-rimed mount back towards the welcome glow of the firelight.

Joe himself was white from head to foot. He climbed wearily out of the saddle, shook himself off, and hunkered close to the flames while Frank attended to his horse.

"Whew!" Joe gave a long sigh of relief as the warmth of the blaze restored his numbed circulation. "Good thing you built this fire, Frank. I was about ready to give up."

"I was hoping you might spot the light," Frank said. "How did we get separated?"

"My carelessness," Joe confessed. "I was looking around for signs of Big Al and sort of trusting my horse to follow yours. First thing I knew, you were nowhere in sight."

The boys blanketed and fed their horses, then opened a can of beans and had a warm supper.

"Wonder if Big Al's lost in the storm, too?" Joe mused drowsily.

"Probably," Frank replied. "If he's smart, he'll find some kind of shelter."

"He may already have found the mine tunnel where Dawson's gold is hidden," Joe pointed out.

"Let's hope not!"

There was a long silence as the two brothers crouched close to the fire, listening to the roar of the storm. Gradually their heads drooped. It was an uneasy, uncomfortable night. Frank and Joe managed to sleep, off and on, but as the fire died down one or the other had to get up and forage for more wood.

With the first clear light of dawn, the brothers were awake and preparing to hit the trail. The snow had stopped sometime during the early morning. Now the whole valley lay covered in a ghostly blanket of white.

"What's our next move?" Joe asked as the boys ate breakfast.

"I think our best bet is to look for the lost plane," Frank suggested. "The mine tunnel can't be too far from there."

Joe shook his head pessimistically. "Don't forget, Big

Al's gang has been looking for it for a long time with no luck."

"But they had nothing to go on," Frank argued. "Of course Dawson's plane fell into a gully—so it might not be too easy to spot."

"That's true," Joe said thoughtfully. "Let's see if we can get some idea of where it came down. According to Dawson, he headed north and was in the air only three or four minutes!"

The Hardys made a rough calculation, based on the probable speed of an old-fashioned single-engine plane. Then, using their compass and taking a bearing on the lone sentinel pine atop the ridge, they started off towards the area where they estimated the crash might have occurred.

The horses could move only at a slow plod. Their forelegs sank knee-deep into the snow at every step. Frank and Joe—their breaths steaming in the sub-zero atmosphere—were forced to control their impatience.

The search continued for several hours. By late morning, both boys were discouraged. Joe, who was in the lead, reined in his horse.

"Seems pretty hopeless, if you ask me," he said, swinging around in his saddle. "Maybe we should—"

Joe broke off with a gasp. As he turned, his eyes had suddenly detected something protruding from the snow in the distance.

"Frank!" Joe pointed off through the clear, cold air.

Frank's eyes widened as he too saw the object. "You're right! Let's go and check!"

Turning their horses, the boys rode towards the spot. Even before they reached it, they could make out the skeletal wing tip of a plane sticking up from a snow-choked gully.

"That's the wreck, all right!" Frank exclaimed jubilantly. "No wonder Big Al and his gang never saw it! Those trees along the edge of the gully would screen it from the ridge!"

The boys halted to discuss the next step in their search.

"The mine tunnel must be somewhere in the mountainside," Frank reasoned. "And it must be on this side of the valley. The other side's miles away—Dawson couldn't have carried the gold that far."

"Which still gives us a lot of ground to cover," Joe said.

The two boys rode towards the edge of the valley where the ground began to slope steeply upward.

"Dawson probably wasn't in good enough shape to climb very far after the crash," Frank said. "So let's concentrate along the lower slopes."

The boys decided to turn left and skirt the mountainside for at least two miles. If their efforts proved fruitless, they would then retrace their steps and try the other direction.

Deep drifts and tangled underbrush made the going difficult. Several times the Hardys were disappointed. What looked like a hole in the mountainside proved to be only the shadow of trees or some rocky outcropping.

But suddenly Frank gave a cry of excitement and pointed. "There's an opening for sure, Joe."

The dark recess was only partly screened by a clump of underbrush. The two boys dismounted, ground-hitched their horses, and scrambled up the slope. They pulled aside the snow-laden brush and Frank shone his flashlight into the hole.

As the yellow beam stabbed through the darkness, Joe murmured, "This looks more like an ordinary cave than a mine tunnel."

"But there *is* a tunnel back there," Frank replied.

In the rear wall of the cavern, about fifty feet or more from the entrance, they could make out another hole which evidently led deep into the mountainside.

"Okay, let's take a look," Joe urged.

The boys entered the cave cautiously and walked towards the inner passage. Frank stopped as he heard a faint rustling noise to their left.

"Hold it, Joe."

His brother turned quickly. A pair of glowing eyes glinted at them from the darkness.

Frank's flashlight revealed an enormous grey wolf! Standing stiffly, the animal glared at the intruders, baring its teeth in a low growl.

Other noises reached the boys' ears. Frank swung his flashlight around and a dozen pairs of wolves' eyes shone in the glow like burning coals.

"Good grief!" Frank's voice was a hoarse whisper. "We've walked straight into a den of wolves!"

· 19 ·

Wolf Prey

FOR a moment the Hardys were paralyzed with fright.

Joe swallowed hard and whispered, "Can we make a break for freedom?"

"We can try."

At the first step, however, the huge timber wolf nearest them gave a savage snarl. The fur on its back bristled stiffly.

Frank muttered, "One false move and that lobo will go for us. This pack acts hungry."

There was a patter of feet in the darkness. The glowing eyes from the dim recesses circled closer. The wolves were gathering around the boys, cutting off escape through the cave entrance!

Frank could feel drops of cold perspiration trickling down his skin. "Snap on your flashlight, too, Joe. That may help hold them back."

Joe played the beam slowly back and forth, while Frank used his.

The wolves slunk restlessly to and fro. Their lolling tongues gave them a wickedly grinning appearance, but they were wary of the lights. Now and then, as a gaunt grey form was caught in the full radiance of a beam, the animal would leap back into the shadows.

It was clear that the flashlights could not hold the beasts at bay for long. As the wolves paced back and forth, the circle was being drawn gradually tighter.

"Watch it!" Joe exclaimed suddenly.

The leader of the pack was advancing straight towards Frank, who stabbed his light full into the wolf's greenish eyes. The brute shrank back, its ears laid flat to its head. A vicious growl issued from its throat.

Instinctively the Hardys moved a step backward. The pack seemed to sense the boys' fear and pressed its advantage, forcing the Hardys to retreat still farther.

"Into the tunnel!" Frank told his brother.

"It may be a blind alley," Joe warned.

"We'll have to risk it—there's no other way out."

Inch by inch, the boys backed towards the tunnel opening.

"It's not wide enough for both of us," Joe said tensely, flashing his light quickly behind them.

"Then you go first," Frank ordered.

They were only a few yards from the tunnel now. Joe began working his way into position behind his brother. The wolves edged closer still, growing bolder, as if they sensed that their victims were trying to escape.

Suddenly the leader gave a vicious snarl and shortened his distance from the boys with a quick leap forward. Again Frank focused his flashlight squarely into the huge beast's eyes—but this time the wolf refused to shrink back. Frank's heart hammered as he saw the bared fangs and slavering jaws. Any instant it would leap in for the kill!

"Quick! A rock!" Frank gasped.

Joe looked around desperately and snatched up a

heavy, jagged stone. He hurled it with all his might at the wolf. The rock hit the beast squarely in the head and the wolf collapsed, with blood oozing from the wound.

A chorus of low growls rose from the pack. The wolves seemed cowed by their leader's downfall, but their nostrils had caught the scent of blood.

"Run for it!" Frank yelled.

Joe turned and plunged into the narrow passageway. Frank followed but more slowly, keeping his light aimed back at the wolves. The pack was gathering around its downed leader, sniffing and growling at the carcass.

Suddenly Frank heard a cry from Joe. It faded abruptly somewhere in the distance.

"Joe! Are you all right?" Frank glanced around hastily but saw only darkness.

A loud snarl drew his attention back towards the main cave. Glowing eyes were peering into the passage as if the wolves were nerving themselves for a renewed attack. Frank backed away fast, hoping to keep them dazzled with the flashlight beam.

Suddenly the ground seemed to end. His foot encountered only empty space!

The next instant Frank was plunging downward through a narrow hole. Instinctively he doubled up and a moment later landed hard amid dirt and rubble.

Frank was breathless from the jolting shock. Luckily he was still clutching the flashlight. He rolled quickly to his feet and played the beam around. A surge of relief swept over him.

Joe was lying on the ground only a few feet away. He, too, had fallen through the hole, but apparently had retained enough presence of mind to roll clear before Frank fell on him.

"Whew!" Joe was struggling for breath. "Had the wind knocked out of me!" As Frank helped him to his feet, he asked, "What about those wolves?"

"Guess they won't bother us down here," Frank replied. He shone his flashlight up the hole, which seemed to be a natural chimney in the rock, but he could see nothing.

Meanwhile, Joe was examining the area into which they had fallen. This too appeared to be a passageway, but larger than the one they had ducked into while escaping from the wolves.

"Frank—look!" Joe exclaimed.

"What's the matter?"

"Timbering!" Joe's beam picked out a few mouldy uprights and crossbeams, still in position at intervals along the passage despite years of disuse. "This place *is* a mine tunnel!"

"You're right!" Frank's voice quivered with excitement. "This must be the tunnel of the Lone Tree diggings that Dawson told us about!"

"Feels like cold air coming from over there," Joe said, glancing towards his right. A curve of the tunnel prevented them from seeing more than ten yards in that direction, but Joe reasoned, "The entrance must be at that end."

Frank agreed and added, "So the chamber with the bluish dirt walls would be the other way. Come on. Let's find out!"

Shining their flashlights ahead, the Hardys plodded on. The tunnel was wide enough for them to proceed

side by side, but at times they had to duck their heads
to avoid bumping them on a crossbeam or a low-
hanging clump of rock. Presently the boys' excitement
grew as they noticed blue-grey streaks appearing in the
earth of the tunnel walls.

"There it is!" Frank cried suddenly.

Far ahead, dimly revealed by the glow of their
flashlights, the tunnel opened out into a wider cavern.
The boys sprinted forward eagerly. As they burst into
the underground chamber, Joe gave a low shout of
triumph.

The walls of the cavern were veined with bluish clay!

"This is the place, all right!" Joe exclaimed.

The Hardys excitedly shone their flashlights around
the chamber. Several rusty picks and shovels lay
scattered about, abandoned by the miners who had
worked there many, many years before. The floor of the
cavern was hard-packed, but in a few moments Frank
and Joe discovered a heap of earth which looked as
though at some time it had been dug up, then replaced.

"Grab a shovel, Joe!" Frank said. "I'll bet this is
where Dawson buried the gold! Let's see if it's still
here!"

Both boys set to work. Though the spot was not
rocky, the digging was difficult. Frank exchanged his
shovel for a pick and began loosening the earth. Then
he switched to a shovel again and helped Joe scoop out
the dislodged dirt and gravel. After several minutes the
Hardys were streaming with perspiration from the
exhausting job.

"Boy! No wonder miners use dynamite!" Joe took off
his heavy jacket. Frank, too, removed his and the boys

returned to the digging. Their flashlights had been propped nearby to illuminate the spot.

Suddenly a yellowish-brown patch showed beneath the dirt. The boys frantically scraped and shovelled away the earth in a frenzy of anticipation.

A moment later they could make out four bulging leather pouches buried in the hole. As Frank beamed his flashlight into it, Joe tipped up a bag. Suddenly one side of the rotting leather burst open and gleaming yellow coins poured from it! The other bags held nuggets.

"Dawson's and Onslow's gold!" Frank cried out.

The boys dropped to their knees, tense with excitement.

"Wow! Imagine how Mike Onslow will feel when he gets the news!" Joe exclaimed.

"He never will!" said a harsh voice directly behind the Hardys.

Frank swung the flashlight around. Not ten feet away stood a glowering man.

"Big Al!" Joe gasped.

"That's right." The gang leader gave an ugly laugh. "Thanks for finding the gold, kids. Too bad you'll never live to enjoy it!"

·20·

Windy Peak Prisoner

"WHAT do you intend to do?" Frank demanded.

"What do *you* think?" Big Al rasped. "I'm going to get rid of you brats for keeps."

"You've tried before," Joe said defiantly.

"I sure have." Big Al's face was hard. "Since your pa's a big detective, I tried to fix you so it would look like an accident. Then I made out like I'd gone over the cliff and got killed. But you punks were still camping there next morning—so I swiped your horses, figuring you'd wind up starved or frozen, and nothing could be pinned on me. That didn't work either."

Frank regarded the outlaw coolly. "So?"

"So now, I've got the gold and that's all that matters. You kids'll never leave here alive." The outlaw's hand went to the holster he was wearing.

"Click off your light, Joe!" Frank said in a whisper, snapping off his own.

As Big Al snaked out his gun, the cavern was plunged into darkness. Frank and Joe dived clear of his line of fire and clawed for their shovels.

The outlaw's gun thundered as both boys hurled their shovels towards the spurt of flame. There was a thud and a cry of pain. At least one of the shovels had found its target.

The boys closed in on Big Al. Frank found the outlaw's gun arm and levered it backwards with both hands. Joe was busy on the other side.

Big Al fought like a madman, but Frank and Joe hung on. The outlaw screeched in pain as Frank applied bone-cracking pressure to his wrist, and a moment later the gun dropped from Big Al's numbed fingers. Frank heard it fall and for an instant slackened pressure as he kicked the revolver out of reach.

The momentary diversion gave Big Al the chance he needed. Digging his fingers into Joe's throat, he hurled the boy hard against the rocky wall. Joe sank to the ground, stunned.

"Now I'll take care of *you*, kid!" Big Al snarled at Frank.

The huge outlaw was more than a match for Frank alone. Frank fought desperately to maintain his hold, but Big Al grabbed his shoulder, jerked him loose, and drove a punch to Frank's face. Frank staggered back, tripped over a rock, and fell heavily to the ground.

"Don't try anything more or I'll beat your brains out!" Big Al warned as he groped for his lost gun.

Meanwhile, Joe had recovered from the pounding Big Al had given him, and was feeling around stealthily for one of the shovels. His fingers closed around a wooden handle just as Big Al spoke. Seizing the implement, Joe sprang to his feet and swung hard in the direction of Big Al's voice.

There was a thudding impact, a gasp, and the sound of a body hitting the ground.

"I got him, Frank!" Joe exclaimed. "Are you all right?"

"Sure—just woozy." Frank pulled himself together and began searching for a flashlight. A moment later he found one and switched it on. Big Al lay stretched on the floor of the cavern, unconscious.

"Good work, Joe! I thought we were goners," Frank confessed, still panting from the struggle. "Let's tie him up before he comes to."

The boys took off their belts and strapped the gang leader's wrists and ankles tightly. Then, with Frank taking his shoulders and Joe his legs, they managed to lug their prisoner through the mine tunnel. The outlaw's roan horse was standing outside, hitched to a rock.

"Stay here and guard him," Frank said to his brother as they dumped their prisoner across the horse's back. "I'll go and get the gold."

Making two trips, Frank hauled out the four bags. Then he stood watch over the unconscious outlaw while Joe went to retrieve their horses.

Joe soon sighted the two animals wandering through the snow along the foot of the mountainside. Evidently the scent of the wolves, or their snarling, had frightened the horses away from the cave.

Joe quickly rounded up their mounts and brought them back to the mouth of the mine tunnel. Big Al had not yet recovered consciousness and Frank was tying him fast to the roan.

"I found some rope in his saddlebag," Frank explained.

The boys loaded the gold into their saddlebags, then

Joe attached the lead rope of Big Al's horse to the saddle of his own mount.

The outlaw was showing signs of reviving. Joe rubbed snow in his face to bring him around faster. As the man's eyes opened, he roared with rage and struggled violently against his bonds. But he soon realized he was helpless.

Big Al's face took on a sullen scowl. "I hope that gold brings you punks and Dawson and Onslow the same kind of bad luck it brought me!" he muttered viciously. "That gold should've been mine twenty-five years ago!"

"You mean when you were Black Pepper, and you and your gang tried to snatch it from those four miners?" Joe asked.

"You know that too, eh?" The outlaw glared at the Hardys. "All right, it's true. I was Black Pepper, and I'd have had the gold if that skunk Dawson hadn't cheated me out of it!"

"*Cheated* you?" Frank retorted sarcastically.

"Because I'd put sand and gravel in the gas tank of his plane. But he managed to take off, and after he crashed a bad storm came up—so we couldn't even find the wreck."

Big Al went on bitterly, "Other jobs came up after that, and I was dodging lawmen. But I never forgot there was a fortune in gold somewhere in these mountains. When my men and I came up here to lie low after that payroll robbery, I figured this was my chance. I'd have had the whole lot if it hadn't been for you!"

"Aren't you forgetting something?" Frank asked. "You'd never have found where Dawson hid the gold if you hadn't overheard us talking at the cabin.

Big Al laughed harshly. "Sure. Even before you two showed up, I was hidin' in the horse shed attached to the cabin and was tryin' to find out what was goin' on. But once I wised up to the fact that Dodge was really Dawson, I'd have choked the truth out of him!"

"Just out of curiosity," Joe said, "how *did* you find the mine today? For that matter, how did you survive the storm?"

"I'm used to this country, kid—found a snug place to hole up for the night," Big Al said boastfully. "This morning I spied your tracks leadin' to that wolf cave. But I spotted the pack before I went barging in. So I searched around and found the real mine tunnel. After that, all I had to do was keep strikin' matches till I saw where the tunnel ended."

"Come on, Joe. We've spent enough time talking," said Frank. "Let's get started!"

The boys knew the trip back to Lucky Lode would be treacherous, especially with a heavy load of gold and the task of keeping a close eye on Big Al. They quickly mounted and started off. Just as the trio emerged from the valley, the Hardys shouted joyfully. They had sighted Hank Shale and Sheriff Kenner topping Lone Tree Ridge!

"Boys! Are you all right?" Hank yelled as he and the sheriff spurred forward to meet them.

Frank and Joe told their story and turned Big Al over to the sheriff. Hank had listened with growing astonishment and admiration.

"You sure are wonders," he said to Frank and Joe. "We were afraid you'd be frozen stiff by now. And here you're bringin' back Big Al *and* the gold! And you solved the mystery o' Bart Dawson!"

"Your pa should be mighty proud of you lads!" Sheriff Kenner added.

The boys grinned and Frank said, "I'm glad we could help out." Then he asked the men, "How did you get here?"

The sheriff explained that after handcuffing Slim and Jake, he and Hank had tried to follow the boys and the fleeing gang leader. But in the darkness, with the other two outlaws on their hands, the chase had proved impossible.

"So we took 'em back to Lucky Lode," said Kenner. "We arrested Burke. He made a full confession about being Slip Gun—the gang's spy in town—and pushing the boulder into Hank's cabin. Later that day we started back to search for you. We looked everywhere and had just given up hope when we ran into Dodge— or Dawson, rather—on his way back and heard part of the story."

"How's Dad?" Frank asked anxiously.

"Doin' fine. Fact is, the doc says he can take the tape off'n his ribs in another day or so," Hank replied. "We practically had to tie him down to keep him from comin' along."

Late that night the lights of Lucky Lode were sighted and by midnight the party rode into town.

Frank and Joe and their father held a warm reunion at Ben Tinker's cabin.

Dawson was also on hand as the boys told their story of finding the gold and capturing Big Al.

"I can't get over it," said Ben Tinker. He chuckled.

"Regardin' you, Dawson, bein' Dodge and you not knowin' it. No wonder you didn't recognize me when I saw you one time up in Helena." Ben cackled with satisfaction. "Reckon now folks'll believe I ain't given to imaginin' things!"

Frank and Joe, glad the case was solved, wondered what kind of adventure would come their way next. They were soon to find out when confronted by *The Mystery of Cabin Island*.

Mr Hardy looked proudly at his sons, then said, "Incidentally, boys, I had a call from Chicago after you left, saying the police had traced that phony taxi driver. Also, those friends of Big Al's, Hopkins and his hoods, were rounded up, thanks to your phone tip. They all just made full confessions. By the way, Hopkins never had a chance to send Onslow's map to Al. The gang was going to pull a bank holdup that afternoon, but your escape ruined their plans."

"Speaking of plans, I wonder what Mike Onslow's will be when he learns he's rich," Frank mused.

Joe chuckled. "Let's phone him first thing in the morning and find out. And I'd give a mint to see Aunt Gertrude's face when *she* hears about the gold!"

Armadas are chosen first by children all over the world. They're pocket-sized and pocket money-sized — and they make terrific presents for friends. They're colourful and exciting and there are hundreds of titles to chose from — baffling mysteries, daring adventures, spine-chilling horror stories, rib-tickling joke books, thrilling stories about schools and ponies — and lots more. Armada has something for everyone.